Whispers from the Realms

AMEYA VATSA

Published by AMEYA VATSA, 2024.

WHISPERS FROM THE REALMS

First edition. September 14, 2024.

ISBN: 979-8227121912

Written by AMEYA VATSA.

Table of Contents

To all the lost souls out there

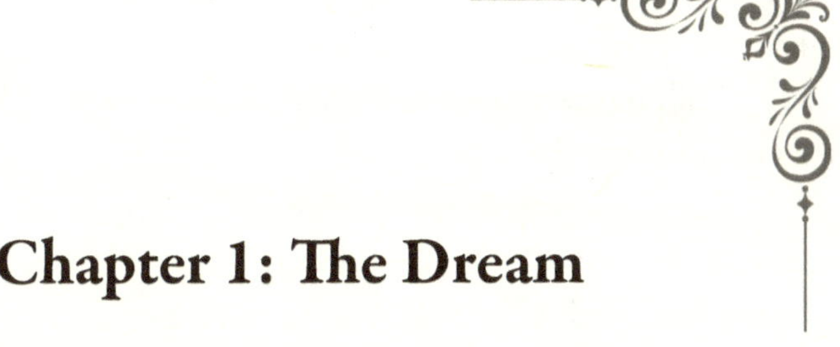

Chapter 1: The Dream

Amara's world was, for the most part, silent. The rhythmic hum of life, the static of daily tasks, and the laughter of friends all seemed muffled, and distant, as though she were walking through life submerged in water. Yet, on the edge of her consciousness, there was always a faint whisper—a sound she couldn't quite grasp. It came most often when she was alone, quiet, and still. But tonight, that whisper grew into something more.

It began like any other night, with Amara lying in bed, her mind buzzing with the remnants of the day. She stared at the ceiling, her fingers curling into the cool fabric of her blanket. She wasn't one to believe in anything spiritual. Life was too busy for such mysteries. Still, her mind refused to let go of the strange feelings she'd been having lately—the sense that she was being watched, that someone or something was trying to reach her.

As her eyes fluttered shut, the transition into the dream was seamless. She found herself standing in a place that felt eerily familiar, though she knew she'd never been there before. It was a vast, open field, covered in a thick fog that swirled around her feet. The sky overhead was a deep, twilight purple, dotted with stars that shimmered like scattered diamonds. A gentle breeze whispered through the fog, carrying with it a sense of peace that filled Amara's heart.

She turned in place, her gaze sweeping across the endless horizon, when she noticed something—someone—standing a short distance away. A tall figure, cloaked in a faint light, beckoned her forward with a wave of his hand.

"Amara," the figure called, though his lips didn't move. The voice echoed in her mind, soft and calming.

She hesitated. Who was this man, and how did he know her name? Curiosity pushed her forward, each step heavy and slow, as though the ground beneath her feet was resisting her movement. The closer she got to the figure, the more details she could make out. His face was obscured by a hood, but there was something about his presence that felt protective—like a guardian watching over her.

"Who are you?" she asked, her voice barely audible in the heavy air.

"I am Kael," he replied, still not moving his lips. The voice was a direct connection to her mind, clear and resonant. "I have been with you for many lifetimes. Do you not remember?"

Amara blinked, confused. "Remember what?"

Kael didn't answer right away. Instead, he reached out his hand, and though she was still several feet away, she felt an intense warmth wash over her, pulling her closer to him. His touch wasn't physical—it was something deeper, something that reached into her very soul. Images began to flash before her eyes—memories that weren't hers, yet felt so deeply familiar. She saw herself in different forms, different lives—one as a healer, another as a seeker of wisdom, and yet another as a leader of her people. But all of it was hazy, distant, like watching shadows dance on a wall.

"You have forgotten, Amara," Kael said softly. "But I am here to help you remember. You have come to this world with a purpose."

Amara's heart pounded in her chest. The memories swirled around her, pulling her deeper into the dream. Her mind struggled to make sense of it all, to grasp onto something solid, but it was like trying to hold onto water. "I don't understand," she whispered. "What is my purpose? What am I supposed to remember?"

Kael's voice was patient, unwavering. "You came to heal, to guide others toward the light. But in this life, you have forgotten. You have become distracted by the noise of the world, the desires of the physical realm. This is not your true path."

The fog around them thickened, swirling faster as Kael's words echoed in the air. Amara felt an overwhelming sense of urgency, like time was running out. Her mind spun, trying to piece together the fragments of her dream, but nothing made sense.

Suddenly, the ground beneath her feet began to tremble. The peaceful landscape started to shift, the stars above flickering out one by one. Fear gripped her chest as the world around her began to disintegrate, the fog pulling away like a veil being lifted from her eyes. She reached out toward Kael, desperate for answers.

"Wait!" she called, her voice trembling. "Don't leave me! I need to know more!"

Kael remained still, his form flickering like a dying flame. "I am always with you," he said, his voice softer now, fading. "But you must learn to listen. The answers are already within you. Seek them, Amara. Remember who you are."

With those final words, the dream collapsed around her. The field, the fog, and Kael all disappeared, leaving her in complete darkness.

Amara's eyes flew open. She gasped for air, her heart racing as though she had just run miles. She was back in her room, the soft glow of the morning sun filtering through the curtains. For a moment, she lay still, staring at the ceiling, trying to shake off the remnants of the dream. Her body felt heavy, her mind clouded with confusion.

Was it just a dream? Or was it something more?

Her hands trembled as she sat up, her eyes darting around the room as though expecting to see Kael standing in the shadows. But there was nothing—just the quiet hum of the city outside her window. Yet, the feeling lingered—the sense that something had shifted, that her life was no longer as simple as it had seemed the day before.

She glanced at the clock on her bedside table. It was 7:00 AM, the start of another ordinary day. But something deep inside her knew that after that dream, nothing would ever be ordinary again.

As she prepared for the day, her thoughts kept drifting back to Kael's words. **"You have come to heal."** What could that possibly mean? And why did it feel so strangely familiar, like a half-forgotten song playing in the background of her mind?

She couldn't shake the feeling that the dream was more than just a product of her imagination. It was as though Kael was real—somehow, somewhere—and he was waiting for her to remember something vital, something that would change the course of her life. But what was it?

For the first time in a long time, Amara felt a pull—a longing for something beyond the everyday noise of life. She didn't know what it was or where it would take her, but one thing was certain: she couldn't ignore it any longer.

The morning unfolded like any other, but Amara moved through it in a daze, her mind still anchored in the dream she couldn't shake off. She rushed through her routine, but nothing felt normal anymore. Everything was charged with an unfamiliar energy, as if the world had subtly shifted overnight. Her body was in autopilot, making breakfast, scrolling through her phone, and catching up on messages, but her mind replayed the vivid dream—Kael's voice, the fog, the overwhelming feeling that something important was missing.

As she stepped out into the world, the hustle and bustle of the city surrounded her. Cars honked, people moved in waves along the streets, and conversations blended into a steady hum. But even amid the noise, Amara felt strangely detached, as if she were standing outside of her own life, observing it from a distance. The dream had left a residue on her spirit, a kind of quiet knowing that made her question the reality around her.

She reached the small coffee shop she frequented every morning before work, a cozy place with soft lighting and a faint smell of roasted beans. The barista greeted her with the usual warmth, but even the simple routine of ordering coffee felt off today. Something was tugging at her, drawing her attention away from the normal rhythms of life.

The bell above the door chimed, signaling a new customer, and Amara absentmindedly glanced in their direction. A man walked in, tall and cloaked in a long coat. There was nothing particularly remarkable about him, yet the sight of him sent a shiver down her spine. He looked familiar, though she couldn't place him. There was a subtle glow about him, almost like the light Kael had carried in her dream.

For a moment, their eyes met. The man's gaze held hers longer than usual, and in that instant, she felt something stir deep inside her. It wasn't just recognition—it was a connection, something beyond words. But before she could make sense of it, he turned away and disappeared into the crowd.

Her coffee was ready, and the barista called her name, jolting her back to the present. Amara shook her head, trying to clear her thoughts. **It's just a coincidence,** she told herself. **It's just because of the dream. I'm overthinking everything.**

But as she walked to her office, strange little coincidences kept happening. The number on the clock when she checked her phone—11:11. A feather that drifted down from the sky, landing directly at her feet. A soft breeze that seemed to whisper her name. Every detail made her pause, like the universe itself was trying to get her attention.

By the time she sat at her desk, the day was already unraveling into a strange blur of signs and symbols. Amara tried to focus on work—emails, meetings, deadlines—but the dream clung to her, seeping into her thoughts like a shadow she couldn't outrun. Kael's voice echoed in the back of her mind, calm and persistent: **"You have forgotten. But I am here to help you remember."**

Remember what? The question nagged at her, frustrating her more with each passing hour. Was it really possible that her life had some deeper, hidden meaning? That her existence was tied to a purpose she had long forgotten? The logical part of her brain dismissed it as nonsense, but another part—one she hadn't listened to in a long time—felt like something profound was stirring beneath the surface of her life.

Later that afternoon, as the sun began to dip behind the city's skyline, Amara decided to take a walk. She often did this when the weight of the day became too much, using the movement to clear her head. Today, however, her steps were driven by something more than stress. She needed answers. Even if they didn't come, she had to at least ask the questions.

She found herself walking toward a quiet park she used to visit, a place she hadn't been in months. The air was cool, the smell of damp earth and fallen leaves thick around her. As she wandered down the winding paths, her thoughts drifted back to Kael, to the words he had spoken. The dream had felt so real, so tangible, like a message she had been waiting to hear for years.

At the edge of the park was a small, secluded bench under a towering oak tree. Amara sat there, staring at the ground, lost in thought. The sounds of the city faded into the background as she closed her eyes, trying to recapture the feeling of the dream, to bring herself back to that place, back to Kael.

For several minutes, she sat in silence, letting the gentle rustling of the leaves soothe her restless mind. It wasn't long before she felt something—a shift in the air, a presence, though invisible, seemed to linger nearby. Her heart quickened, and for a moment, she wondered if she was just imagining it.

And then, the whisper came.

"Amara…"

Her eyes shot open, and she scanned the park, her breath catching in her throat. There was no one there—at least, not physically. But the voice had been unmistakable. It wasn't an external sound; it was something deeper, a vibration within her soul, a voice that bypassed her ears entirely.

"Kael?" she whispered back, feeling ridiculous, but the moment was too intense to ignore.

There was no reply, but the wind picked up, swirling the fallen leaves around her feet. The world felt charged, alive with something she couldn't see but could undeniably feel. It was as if the boundaries between her world and something greater were thinning, if only for a moment.

She didn't know how long she sat there, but when the sensation finally faded, Amara felt both exhilarated and unnerved. Something was happening—something beyond her control, beyond her understanding. And she couldn't deny it anymore.

The walk home was quiet, her thoughts swirling with the events of the day. By the time she reached her apartment, she felt exhausted, emotionally and spiritually drained. As she opened the door and stepped inside, she was met with the familiar comfort of home—the soft lighting, the smell of lavender from the diffuser, the faint sound of classical music playing in the background.

Yet, despite the calmness of her surroundings, Amara knew that her life was no longer the same. The dream had opened a door, and something had crossed through—a force she couldn't ignore.

Before going to bed, she grabbed a notebook from her desk, something she hadn't used in years. Sitting on the edge of her bed, she began to write. Her handwriting was hurried, messy, but the words flowed effortlessly. She wrote about Kael, about the dream, about the strange coincidences that had followed her throughout the day. As she wrote, a question began to form in the back of her mind, one that scared her more than anything else: **What if everything I know about life is wrong?**

When she finished writing, she closed the notebook and set it on the bedside table. Exhausted, she slipped under the covers and closed her eyes, half-expecting another dream to pull her into the spiritual realm once more. But sleep came quickly, and this time, it was dreamless.

Amara had no idea what tomorrow would bring, but for the first time in a long time, she felt like she was on the edge of something bigger than herself. A journey had begun, whether she was ready for it or not.

Chapter 2: The Forgotten Purpose

The days after the dream passed in a haze. Amara went through the motions—wake up, work, come home, repeat—but everything felt off-kilter. There was an emptiness in her chest, as if she were walking through a hollow version of her life. No matter how much she tried to focus, her thoughts constantly wandered back to Kael and the dream. His voice, the calm authority in his words, echoed in her mind at the oddest moments.

You have come to heal.

But heal what? Heal whom? Amara felt like she was searching for something she couldn't name. The sense of disconnection grew stronger with each passing day. No matter how hard she tried to ignore it, there was an unmistakable longing for something she couldn't quite place, like a melody playing just out of reach.

At work, the once comforting routine of emails, meetings, and deadlines now seemed utterly meaningless. Each time she sat down at her desk, she felt the same nagging sensation—the growing emptiness of a life lived without purpose. She found herself staring at her computer screen, her mind wandering far beyond the office walls. It was as though her soul was yearning for something bigger, something deeper than the constant churn of the corporate grind.

Even her friends noticed the change. "You seem distracted lately," one of her colleagues mentioned during lunch, concern lacing her words. "Are you alright?"

Amara nodded absently, giving her usual half-smile. "Yeah, I'm fine. Just tired, I guess."

But she wasn't fine. Deep down, she knew it.

One evening, nearly two weeks after the dream, Amara found herself walking aimlessly through the city streets. She had taken this route many times before, but tonight, the city felt foreign, like a backdrop to a play in which she no longer had a role. She drifted past restaurants and shops, her mind a thousand miles away.

What am I missing? she thought, the question looping endlessly in her mind. **Why do I feel like there's something I'm supposed to be doing, but I can't remember what it is?**

The more she thought about it, the more frustrated she became. The dream had shaken something loose inside her, some forgotten part of herself that she had no idea how to reclaim. It was maddening, this sense of being on the edge of a discovery, yet not knowing where to look.

She wandered into a park she hadn't visited in months, the tall trees casting long shadows across the quiet paths. The air was cool, crisp, and carried with it the scent of autumn leaves. There was something soothing about the stillness here, the way the world seemed to slow down. Amara sat on a bench near the edge of a small pond, the water rippling softly in the fading light.

She closed her eyes and took a deep breath, trying to quiet her restless mind. But the moment her thoughts began to settle, that familiar presence returned—the same feeling she had experienced in the dream. It was faint at first, a soft stirring in the air around her, like the gentle brush of invisible wings.

And then came the whisper.

"Amara..."

Her eyes shot open, her heart pounding in her chest. She looked around, half expecting to see Kael standing nearby, but the park was empty. The voice hadn't come from outside—it had come from within her. It was soft, distant, but unmistakable. It was Kael.

Amara... The whisper was stronger now, more insistent. **You must remember.**

"Remember what?" she whispered back, her voice trembling. "What am I supposed to remember?"

But there was no reply. The presence faded, leaving Amara alone with her confusion. She buried her face in her hands, frustration welling up inside her. It was like trying to solve a puzzle with half the pieces missing.

After a few moments, she stood up and began walking again, the weight of her thoughts pressing down on her shoulders. The dream, the whispers—it was all too much. She didn't know how to make sense of any of it.

Later that night, as she lay in bed staring at the ceiling, her mind refused to quiet down. The whispers, the memories of Kael, the signs—it all pointed to something just beyond her reach. But no matter how hard she tried, she couldn't grasp it.

Amara tossed and turned, sleep eluding her as her thoughts spiraled deeper into frustration. **What am I supposed to do?** she thought over and over again. **What is my purpose?**

Finally, after what felt like hours of wrestling with her thoughts, exhaustion overtook her, and she drifted off into a fitful sleep.

That night, the dreams came again, but this time they were different. The peaceful field and the soothing presence of Kael were gone, replaced by something darker, more chaotic.

Amara found herself standing in the middle of a storm. Lightning flashed in the sky, and the wind howled around her, pulling at her clothes and hair. She struggled to stay on her feet as the ground beneath her shook, cracks forming in the earth, threatening to swallow her whole.

"Kael!" she screamed into the chaos. "Where are you?"

But there was no answer.

Suddenly, a figure appeared in the distance, barely visible through the swirling storm. It was Malek. His silhouette loomed in the darkness, his form flickering like a ghost. His eyes glowed faintly, filled with a sorrow that pierced Amara's heart.

"You must find your way," Malek's voice echoed in the storm, distorted by the wind. "Or you will be lost, just like I was."

"I don't understand!" Amara shouted back, her voice desperate. "What am I supposed to do?"

The wind grew stronger, and Malek's figure began to fade, his words barely audible now. "Remember who you are, Amara. Before it's too late."

The ground beneath her crumbled, and Amara felt herself falling, plunging into the darkness below. She screamed, her heart racing as the blackness swallowed her whole.

Amara awoke with a jolt, her body drenched in sweat, her heart hammering in her chest. She gasped for air, the remnants of the dream still clinging to her. For a moment, she lay there, disoriented, her mind struggling to separate dream from reality.

Malek's words echoed in her ears: **"You must find your way. Or you will be lost, just like I was."**

The fear in his voice had been palpable, as if he were warning her of something imminent, something she couldn't afford to ignore.

Amara sat up in bed, her mind racing. She couldn't keep going like this—living in a fog, unsure of what she was meant to do. The signs, the whispers, the dreams—they were all pushing her toward something. And now, more than ever, she felt the urgency to figure it out.

She threw off the covers and got out of bed, her hands trembling. **I need to do something,** she thought. **I can't keep ignoring this.**

Without thinking, she grabbed her notebook from the bedside table and began writing, her pen moving furiously across the page. She wrote about the dreams, about Malek, about Kael's voice in the park. She wrote about the growing sense of urgency, the feeling that her life was slipping away from her, that she was meant for something more but couldn't remember what it was.

When she finally stopped writing, her hands were shaking, and her heart was pounding in her chest. She stared at the pages in front of her, the words blurred by the tears that had started to fall.

"I don't want to be lost," she whispered to herself. "I need to remember."

But even as the words left her lips, she knew that the path ahead wouldn't be easy. There were still so many questions, so many unknowns. And the fear of losing herself, of becoming like Malek, haunted her.

As the first light of dawn crept through her window, Amara knew that she couldn't go back to living her life the way she had before. Something had changed. Something had awakened inside her.

And now, there was no turning back.

Amara's mind raced as she scribbled furiously in her notebook. The words tumbled out like a flood, a rush of thoughts she had been holding back for days. Her hand ached, but she couldn't stop—she had to get it all down, every detail, every moment that had led her to this strange and terrifying point.

She wrote about the dream, about Kael's voice, about the feeling that had clung to her ever since that night. The feeling that something was pulling her, guiding her toward something she couldn't yet see. But the words didn't bring her peace. If anything, they heightened the confusion swirling in her mind.

She sat back, looking at the scrawled pages in front of her. The ink was smudged where her tears had fallen, and she couldn't help but wonder what had happened to her life. Just weeks ago, everything had been so normal, so predictable. Work, friends, weekends spent in the city—it had all felt routine, safe. Now, she felt like a stranger in her own life, adrift in a sea of unanswered questions.

The dreams had started to feel more real than her waking life. And it wasn't just the dreams. It was the signs, the whispers in the park, the subtle things she noticed throughout the day. The world had taken on a different texture, as though she were seeing it through new eyes, or perhaps through ancient eyes that had been waiting for her to awaken.

The next morning, Amara woke early, the echoes of her dream still fresh in her mind. Malek's words hung over her like a dark cloud. **"You must find your way. Or you will be lost, just like I was."** There was something about him, something broken, that scared her.

She spent the morning trying to shake off the unease, but no matter how hard she tried, the sense of dread stayed with her. It wasn't just Malek's warning—it was the realization that she might be wandering down the same path. She could feel herself slipping, losing her connection to something she couldn't even name.

She stared out of her apartment window, watching as the city woke up, people bustling about their lives, seemingly unaware of the deeper currents that ran beneath the surface. **Am I the only one who feels this?** she wondered. **Does anyone else notice the way the world shifts, the way time feels like it's pulling us toward something inevitable?**

She couldn't help but think about her co-workers, her friends, the people she saw every day. They all seemed so grounded, so sure of themselves. But now, Amara couldn't shake the feeling that they, too, were forgetting something. Something important.

Her phone buzzed, pulling her from her thoughts. It was a message from Jessica, one of her closest friends.

Hey! Haven't seen you in a while. Drinks tonight?

Amara stared at the message for a long moment, her fingers hovering over the keyboard. Normally, she would have jumped at the chance to see her friends, to unwind after a long week. But now, the thought of going out, pretending everything was fine, felt impossible. She wasn't fine. She hadn't been fine in weeks. But how could she explain that to anyone?

Finally, she typed a reply.

Can't tonight. Not feeling well.

The lie tasted bitter on her tongue, but she didn't know what else to say. She wasn't ready to talk about what was happening, not yet. Not until she understood it herself.

That afternoon, Amara found herself walking through the park again, the same path she had taken so many times before. The wind was colder today, a sharp edge to the air that made her pull her jacket tighter around her. The leaves had turned a deep shade of amber, and they crunched beneath her boots as she walked.

There was something about the park that always made her feel more connected, more grounded. Maybe it was the quiet, the way the noise of the city seemed to fade into the background here. Or maybe it was the memories. She had come here often as a child, running through the trees, her imagination alive with stories of magical worlds hidden just beyond the trees.

But now, it wasn't just her imagination. The magic she had once pretended to believe in felt real, palpable. She could feel it in the air, in the way the wind seemed to speak to her, in the way the leaves rustled as if in conversation. She had always sensed something more in the world, something unseen, but now it was undeniable.

As she reached the bench by the pond, she sat down, staring at the water as it rippled softly in the breeze. For a long time, she just sat there, listening, waiting. She wasn't sure what she was waiting for, but the park felt like the right place to be. It felt like a place where answers might find her, if only she could stay still long enough to hear them.

Minutes passed, and the world around her seemed to slow, the sounds of the city fading into the distance. Her breath became steady, her mind quieting for the first time in days.

And then, just as before, she felt it—the presence. The air around her seemed to shift, as though something invisible had brushed past her. Her heart quickened, but this time, she didn't panic. She closed her eyes, focusing on the feeling, letting it fill her. The warmth, the sense of being watched over. It was Kael. She knew it was.

"Amara..." The voice was softer this time, more distant, but still clear.

"I'm here," she whispered, her voice barely audible. "I'm listening."

The wind picked up, swirling around her, and for a moment, she thought she could almost see him—Kael, standing just beyond the edge of her vision, his form shimmering like light through fog. But before she could make out his face, the image flickered and faded, leaving her alone once more.

Her heart pounded in her chest, and she felt a rush of emotion—fear, hope, longing. The connection had been so fleeting, but it was there. It was real.

"I don't understand," she whispered to the wind. "What am I supposed to do? How do I remember?"

But there was no answer, only the rustling of the leaves as the wind died down.

As the days passed, Amara continued to feel the pull of something greater. She spent hours reading, searching through books on spirituality, ancient wisdom, and the nature of the soul. None of it felt new to her—it was as if she had known these things once, in another time, another life, and was now rediscovering them piece by piece.

She found herself waking in the middle of the night, her mind racing with thoughts and questions. She scribbled in her notebook by the faint glow of her bedside lamp, trying to capture the ideas before they slipped away. The dreams continued, though they were less vivid now, more like glimpses of something just beyond her reach. Each morning, she woke with a sense of urgency, as though time were running out.

One night, as she lay in bed staring at the ceiling, her phone buzzed with an incoming call. It was her mother. Amara hesitated for a moment before answering. She hadn't spoken to her mother in days, and the thought of a conversation felt exhausting. But something inside her urged her to pick up.

"Hi, Mom," she said, trying to keep her voice steady.

"Amara, are you okay?" her mother's voice was soft, but there was an edge of concern. "I've been worried about you."

Amara sighed, closing her eyes. "Yeah, I'm fine. Just...tired, I guess."

There was a pause on the other end of the line. "You don't sound fine, sweetheart. Is something going on? You know you can talk to me."

Amara felt a lump form in her throat. How could she explain what she was going through? How could she put into words the strange pull she felt, the way her life seemed to be unraveling in ways she couldn't control?

"I don't know, Mom," she said, her voice cracking. "I just... I feel like I'm lost. Like I don't know who I am anymore."

There was silence for a long moment, and then her mother's voice came, gentle but firm. "Amara, you've always known who you are. Maybe you've just forgotten for a little while. But I know you. You'll find your way."

Her mother's words hit her like a wave, and Amara felt tears welling up in her eyes. **You'll find your way.** It was exactly what Malek had said. But this time, coming from her mother, it felt like a promise.

As the conversation ended, Amara lay in the dark, her mind still swirling with thoughts. Her mother's words had given her a sense of comfort, but they hadn't erased the fear that lingered deep inside her. She was still lost. She still didn't know how to remember the things she was supposed to.

But maybe, she thought, remembering wasn't something that could be forced. Maybe it was something that would come to her when she was ready. And until then, she would have to keep searching, keep listening to the whispers of her soul.

With that thought, Amara closed her eyes, the weight of the past few weeks finally lifting from her shoulders, if only a little. There was still a long road ahead, but for the first time in a long time, she didn't feel quite so alone.

Chapter 3: Meeting Malek

The dreams had begun to take on a life of their own. Each night, Amara would drift into a world that felt more real than anything she experienced during the day. There was a weight to the air, a sense of urgency that pressed in on her from all sides. She could no longer deny that something was happening—something she couldn't control. Her connection to the unseen world was deepening, and the veil between her life and the spirit realm was thinning.

It had been weeks since she first heard Kael's voice, and though the dreams of him had grown quieter, something else had taken their place. Someone else.

That night, Amara found herself standing in a vast, open space. The ground beneath her feet was dark and cold, a glossy black surface that stretched on for miles in every direction. The sky above was a swirling mix of shadows and light, a storm on the verge of breaking. She was alone, or at least, she thought she was.

Then, in the distance, a figure appeared. Tall, thin, and cloaked in shadows, the figure moved slowly toward her, as though carried by the wind. Amara's heart raced as she recognized him—it was Malek, the lost soul she had seen in her dreams before. His presence was different from Kael's. Where Kael had radiated warmth and light, Malek was a void, a being of cold shadows that seemed to pull the light from the air around him.

Amara's first instinct was to run, to flee from whatever it was that Malek represented. But something held her in place. Despite the fear creeping up her spine, she felt drawn to him, as though there was something he had to tell her, something important.

As he approached, his form flickered, shifting in and out of focus like a dying flame. His face was gaunt, hollow, his eyes glowing faintly with a sadness that seemed to stretch back through lifetimes. He stopped a few feet from her, his gaze locking onto hers.

"You're still here," he said, his voice low and haunting. "Still clinging to this life, searching for answers."

Amara swallowed hard, her throat dry. "Who are you?" she asked, though she already knew the answer. "What do you want from me?"

Malek's lips curled into a bitter smile. "I was like you once. Full of purpose, full of life. But I forgot. I lost my way. And now..." His voice trailed off, and he looked away, his eyes darkening. "Now, I am nothing. A shadow of what I was."

Amara felt a chill run through her. "What happened to you?"

Malek's gaze returned to hers, and in his eyes, she saw a deep, aching sorrow. "I forgot my purpose. I became lost in the distractions of the world—the noise, the desires, the fears. I ignored the signs, ignored the voice inside me that told me what I was meant to do. And by the time I realized what I had lost, it was too late."

He took a step closer, and Amara instinctively backed away, her heart pounding in her chest.

"I'm warning you," Malek said, his voice like the wind in a graveyard. "You're on the same path. You're drifting, forgetting what you came here to do. If you don't wake up, if you don't remember, you will end up like me. A lost soul, wandering between worlds, forever searching for what cannot be found."

Amara's mind raced. Could that really happen to her? Could she forget her purpose so completely that she would lose herself forever?

"But I don't know what I'm supposed to do," she said, her voice barely a whisper. "I don't remember."

Malek's expression softened, just for a moment. "You will," he said. "But only if you start listening. The signs are all around you. The whispers, the dreams—they're trying to guide you, to help you remember. But you must choose to follow them."

Amara stared at him, her heart heavy with the weight of his words. She wanted to believe him, wanted to believe that there was still time for her to find her way. But the fear gnawed at her, the fear that it was already too late.

"Is that why you're here?" she asked, her voice trembling. "To warn me?"

Malek's gaze darkened once more. "I'm here because I've been watching you. Because you remind me of who I used to be. You still have a chance, Amara. But if you don't wake up soon, you will lose that chance. And once it's gone..." He shook his head. "There's no getting it back."

Amara woke with a start, her heart pounding in her chest. The room was dark, the only sound the faint hum of the city outside her window. She sat up, running a hand through her hair, her mind spinning. Malek's words echoed in her ears, a warning that felt all too real.

You're drifting. You're forgetting.

For the first time in weeks, the fear wasn't something distant, something she could push aside. It was real, tangible, a weight pressing down on her. She could no longer ignore the signs, no longer pretend that everything was fine. Something inside her was changing, and if she didn't figure out what it was, she feared she would lose herself completely.

She got out of bed and crossed the room to the window, staring out at the city lights below. The world was so alive, so full of noise and distraction. It was easy to lose oneself in it, to forget the deeper truths that lay hidden beneath the surface. But Amara couldn't afford to forget anymore.

She had to wake up.

The next morning, Amara moved through her day in a daze. The dream with Malek had shaken her to her core, and she couldn't stop thinking about his warning. Every time she caught a glimpse of her reflection in a window or mirror, she saw the fear in her own eyes—the fear that she was already on the path to becoming lost.

At work, her focus was non-existent. Emails went unanswered, meetings drifted by in a blur, and her co-workers' conversations seemed distant, like echoes in a cave. She felt disconnected from everything, as though she were a ghost moving through the motions of someone else's life.

By lunchtime, she couldn't take it anymore. She grabbed her coat and left the office, needing to escape the suffocating atmosphere. She walked through the city streets, her mind racing, her thoughts a jumbled mess of confusion and fear.

What am I supposed to do? she thought, over and over again. **How do I wake up?**

She found herself back at the park, the place that had always brought her some measure of peace. But today, the park felt different. The trees loomed taller, their branches casting long shadows across the ground. The air was thick with tension, as though the world itself was holding its breath.

Amara sat on her usual bench by the pond, staring at the water as it rippled softly in the breeze. Her heart ached with the weight of everything she didn't understand, everything she couldn't remember. She wanted so badly to wake up, to remember what she was meant to do. But no matter how hard she tried, the answers remained just out of reach.

She closed her eyes, taking a deep breath, and tried to calm her racing mind. She had to listen. That's what Malek had said. The signs were all around her. She just had to listen.

For several minutes, she sat in silence, focusing on the sounds of the park—the rustling of the leaves, the distant hum of the city, the soft lapping of the water against the shore. And then, just as before, she felt it—that presence, that warmth.

"Amara..."

Her eyes flew open, and there, standing by the edge of the pond, was Kael. His form shimmered in the soft light, his face calm and reassuring. He didn't say anything, but his presence was enough. The fear that had been gripping her heart began to ease, replaced by a sense of peace she hadn't felt in weeks.

"Kael," she whispered, her voice trembling. "What am I supposed to do? How do I remember?"

Kael's gaze softened, and though he didn't speak, Amara understood. The answers weren't something she could find by searching outside herself. They were inside her, waiting to be discovered. But she had to be patient. She had to trust.

And so, for the first time in a long time, Amara let go. She stopped fighting, stopped searching, and simply listened.

And in the silence, she began to remember.

Amara sat on the bench in the park long after Kael's presence had faded. The calm that had briefly washed over her ebbed away, leaving her with the same unsettling feeling of being on the edge of something monumental but terrifying. She wanted to trust Kael's reassurance, to believe that the answers were within her, but the fear still lingered.

What if she never remembered? What if she was doomed to walk through life in this fog, never fully realizing her purpose?

The encounter with Malek had shaken her deeply. His warning haunted her thoughts—**"You will be lost, just like I was."** There was a bitterness in his voice, a rawness that hinted at a life full of regret. Amara didn't know the full story of how he had lost his way, but she felt the weight of his pain. It was a fate she feared more than anything.

As she walked home that evening, the city felt colder than usual. The busy streets, filled with people going about their lives, suddenly seemed distant. Amara felt like an outsider looking in, as though she no longer belonged to the same world as everyone else. The connection to the spirit world had changed her, made her acutely aware of how fragile and temporary the material world was.

The signs were still there, too—the synchronicities, the whispers, the feeling that something or someone was always watching. It was unnerving, but she couldn't ignore it anymore. She couldn't pretend her life was normal when everything about it had changed.

When she arrived home, the first thing she did was reach for her notebook. She had been writing feverishly since the dreams started, trying to capture every detail, every feeling. Her notebook had become her lifeline, a way to process the strange new reality she was living in.

She flipped through the pages, reading over her scattered thoughts from the past few weeks. The words were a mess of confusion, desperation, and longing. But one thing was clear: she was on a journey, and there was no turning back.

Over the next few days, Amara became more and more withdrawn from her everyday life. She stopped going out with friends, avoided social events, and even found herself skipping work on occasion. Her world had narrowed down to the dreams, the whispers, and her constant search for meaning.

It was late one night, after another restless sleep, that she felt the pull to return to the park. The dreams with Malek had become more frequent, more intense. Every time, he seemed more desperate, more insistent that she listen to him. The cold emptiness of his presence contrasted sharply with the warmth she felt from Kael, and she didn't know which path she was supposed to follow.

That night, the air was thick with an unnatural stillness. The park was almost eerily quiet, the usual sounds of rustling leaves and distant city noise muffled. Amara's steps felt heavier as she made her way to her usual spot by the pond. The moon hung low in the sky, casting a pale light over the water, making the surface shimmer like glass.

She sat on the bench, her eyes fixed on the reflection of the moon in the water. It felt as though time had slowed, the world around her waiting for something to happen.

And then, out of the corner of her eye, she saw him.

Malek stood at the edge of the pond, his form barely visible in the shadows. His eyes glowed faintly, the same sadness etched into his face. This time, though, he seemed more solid, more present than before.

"You came," he said, his voice carrying on the still air.

Amara's heart raced, but she forced herself to stay calm. "Why do you keep coming to me?" she asked, her voice steady. "What do you want?"

Malek's eyes darkened. "It's not what I want. It's what you need to understand."

He took a step closer, and Amara felt a chill creep up her spine. There was something about him that both terrified and fascinated her. His presence was heavy, oppressive, like a storm about to break.

"You're drifting," Malek continued, his voice low. "Just like I did. You're letting the world pull you in different directions, away from the truth. Away from who you're supposed to be."

Amara's hands gripped the edge of the bench. "I'm trying to understand," she said, her voice filled with frustration. "But I don't know how. I don't know what I'm supposed to do."

Malek's face twisted into a grimace. "That's exactly the problem. You're waiting for the answers to come to you, but they won't. You have to choose, Amara. You have to make a decision about who you want to be."

His words hit her like a blow. A decision. That was what had been haunting her all along—the knowledge that she had to take control of her life, that no one else could do it for her. But the fear of making the wrong choice, of following the wrong path, had kept her frozen.

"What if I choose wrong?" she whispered, her voice barely audible.

Malek's gaze softened, just for a moment. "There's no right or wrong path, Amara. There's only the path you walk. But if you do nothing, if you keep drifting, you will lose yourself. Just like I did."

Amara's breath caught in her throat. She could feel the weight of his words, the truth in them. But there was something else, something he wasn't telling her.

"What happened to you?" she asked, her voice trembling. "How did you lose your way?"

For a long moment, Malek didn't answer. He turned away, staring out at the pond, his expression unreadable.

"I forgot who I was," he finally said, his voice barely above a whisper. "I let the world consume me. I let fear and doubt take over. And by the time I realized what I had lost, it was too late."

Amara's heart ached at the sadness in his voice. She didn't know Malek's full story, but she could feel the weight of his regret, the pain of a soul that had wandered too far from the light.

"I don't want to end up like you," she said softly.

Malek turned to her, his eyes burning with intensity. "Then wake up, Amara. Wake up before it's too late."

The encounter with Malek left Amara feeling raw and vulnerable. She had always known, deep down, that she was drifting, but hearing it from him made it all too real. She was terrified of losing herself, of becoming like him—a soul forever wandering, searching for a purpose that could never be regained.

But how was she supposed to wake up? How was she supposed to remember who she was?

That night, as she lay in bed, she tried to focus on Kael's words. **"The answers are within you."** But every time she closed her eyes, all she could see was Malek's face, his hollow eyes, his warning.

She tossed and turned, unable to find peace. Sleep came in fitful waves, each dream more disjointed than the last. When she finally drifted off, she found herself once again in the dark, cold space where Malek had first appeared.

But this time, Kael was there, too.

He stood at a distance, watching her with his calm, knowing eyes. His presence brought a sense of warmth and safety, a stark contrast to the oppressive cold that surrounded Malek.

"You're not alone, Amara," Kael said, his voice steady. "I've always been with you. But you must choose to listen."

Amara looked between Kael and Malek, the two figures representing the choices that lay before her. Kael, the guide who had always been there, patiently waiting for her to wake up. And Malek, the cautionary tale, the soul who had lost his way.

"I don't know what to do," she said, her voice trembling.

Kael stepped forward, his gaze soft but firm. "You do. You just have to trust yourself."

When Amara awoke the next morning, she felt different. The fear was still there, but it was accompanied by something else—an awareness, a clarity she hadn't felt before. She didn't have all the answers, but she knew that waiting for them wasn't the solution. She had to start making decisions, start trusting herself.

Malek's warning echoed in her mind, but so did Kael's reassurance. The path ahead was unclear, but she wasn't lost. Not yet.

Chapter 4: The Karmic Web

Amara had always heard people talk about karma—the cosmic balance between actions and their consequences. But to her, it had always been a vague concept, something spiritual gurus and self-help books referenced but never something she truly understood. Until now.

Since the night in the park with Malek, everything had taken on a new weight. His words, his warning—they had forced her to confront the reality of her choices. For the first time in her life, Amara couldn't run from the truth that had been pressing in on her for weeks. She was responsible for the direction of her soul, for the decisions that had shaped her life. And now, it seemed, the universe was making sure she understood that lesson.

It was early morning when the dreams returned. Amara had spent another sleepless night, tossing and turning as she tried to make sense of everything that had happened. She had drifted off just before dawn, exhausted from the mental and emotional strain.

This time, the dream was different. Instead of the cold, dark space she had come to associate with Malek, she found herself in a vast, open field. The grass was tall and golden, swaying gently in a warm breeze. The sky above was a deep shade of blue, with clouds drifting lazily across it. The scene was peaceful, serene—almost too perfect.

Amara stood in the middle of the field, looking around, trying to understand where she was. In the distance, she saw a figure approaching, walking slowly through the tall grass. Her heart raced as she recognized the figure—it was Kael.

He moved with a calm, purposeful grace, his presence as reassuring as ever. When he reached her, he smiled softly, his eyes filled with the same wisdom she had come to expect from him.

"Amara," he said gently, "you've come far, but there is still much for you to see. Much for you to understand."

Amara's brow furrowed. "I don't know what I'm supposed to do," she admitted. "I'm trying to listen, to understand, but it's like the answers are just out of reach."

Kael nodded, his expression sympathetic. "That's because you're still looking for the answers outside of yourself. But everything you need is within you. The choices you've made, the paths you've taken—they are all connected. Every action, every decision, has led you to this moment."

He gestured to the field around them, and suddenly, the landscape shifted. The golden grass faded, replaced by scenes from Amara's life—moments she recognized, and others she didn't. Faces flashed before her, people she had known, people she had loved, and people she had wronged. It was overwhelming, like watching a movie of her own life play out in fast motion.

Amara turned to Kael, her heart pounding. "What is this?"

Kael's eyes darkened slightly, the gravity of the moment settling in. "This is the karmic web, Amara. The choices you've made in this life and in the lives before it. Each decision has consequences, each action ripples through time, creating connections, debts, and lessons that must be learned."

Amara stared at the shifting scenes, her mind reeling. She saw herself as a child, stealing from a friend out of jealousy. She saw herself as a young adult, ignoring someone in need because she was too wrapped up in her own problems. But then, the images changed. They became more distant, unfamiliar, and yet deeply personal.

She saw herself in different bodies, in different eras. She was a healer in one life, a scholar in another. She watched herself make decisions that seemed small at the time but had profound consequences. In one life, she was a woman who had refused to help her village during a time of crisis. In another, she was a man who had sacrificed his own life to save others. Each scene felt both foreign and familiar, like memories she had forgotten but were still a part of her.

"I've... lived all these lives?" Amara asked, her voice trembling.

Kael nodded. "You are more than this one life, Amara. You've lived many, and each one has taught you something. But with each life, there are choices left unresolved, lessons left unlearned. That is why you are here now. To continue learning, to resolve what was left unfinished."

Amara felt a wave of emotion wash over her—regret, fear, and a deep sense of responsibility. "What am I supposed to do with all of this?" she asked, her voice barely above a whisper.

Kael stepped closer, his presence warm and reassuring. "You must understand that the choices you make now are not isolated. They are part of the larger web, connected to everything that has come before and everything that will come after. The people you encounter, the challenges you face—they are all opportunities for you to learn and to heal."

He paused, his gaze softening. "But you must also understand that not all debts are yours to pay. Some souls carry their own karmic weight, and it is not your responsibility to fix everything. You are here to grow, to evolve, and to help others where you can. But you cannot lose yourself in the process."

Amara's mind raced as she tried to take in everything Kael was telling her. The idea that her actions, both in this life and in past lives, had created a web of consequences was overwhelming. She thought back to the decisions she had made, the people she had hurt, and the ways she had failed to live up to her potential.

"But what if I've made too many mistakes?" she asked, her voice cracking with emotion. "What if I've done too much damage?"

Kael's expression remained gentle. "There are no mistakes, Amara. Only lessons. Every action, every decision, is an opportunity to learn. And you are here now because you are ready to understand that."

He reached out, placing a hand on her shoulder. "You are not defined by your past. You are defined by the choices you make now, in this moment. The past has brought you here, but it does not have to determine your future."

Amara closed her eyes, taking a deep breath. The weight of her past actions still pressed down on her, but Kael's words brought a glimmer of hope. Maybe she wasn't beyond saving. Maybe there was still time to set things right.

The scene around them shifted again, and Amara found herself standing in a darkened room. In the center of the room was a large, glowing web, shimmering with light. Threads of energy stretched out from the web, connecting to different points in the room, each one representing a choice, a decision, a life.

"This is the karmic web," Kael said, his voice low and reverent. "It connects all souls, all actions. Each thread is a choice, each connection is a consequence."

Amara stepped closer to the web, her eyes wide with wonder. The threads pulsed with energy, some bright and vibrant, others dim and frayed. She could feel the weight of each thread, the energy of every decision made.

Kael moved to stand beside her. "Every action creates a thread, and every thread connects to another. Some are strong, others are weak. But all are part of the web."

Amara reached out, her fingers brushing one of the glowing threads. As soon as she touched it, a wave of emotion washed over her—regret, guilt, sorrow. She saw a vision of herself in a past life, making a choice that had hurt others. The pain of that choice still lingered in the thread, unresolved, waiting to be healed.

She pulled her hand back, her heart heavy. "I didn't realize..."

Kael nodded. "Most souls don't. But now you do. And that is the first step toward healing."

The vision began to fade, and Amara found herself standing in the field once more. The weight of the karmic web still pressed on her, but there was a sense of clarity now, a deeper understanding of the choices she had made and the ones she still had to make.

Kael stood beside her, his presence steady and comforting. "You are not alone in this, Amara. The web is vast, and it connects all souls. But you are never alone."

Amara nodded, her mind still reeling from everything she had seen. "Thank you," she said softly, her voice filled with gratitude.

Kael smiled, his eyes warm. "The journey is just beginning. But you are ready."

Amara woke with a sense of peace she hadn't felt in weeks. The dream, the vision of the karmic web, had given her a new perspective on her life, on her choices. She still had a long way to go, but for the first time, she felt like she was on the right path.

The lessons of her past lives, the connections she had made, the debts she still had to resolve—it was all part of the journey. And now, she was ready to face it.

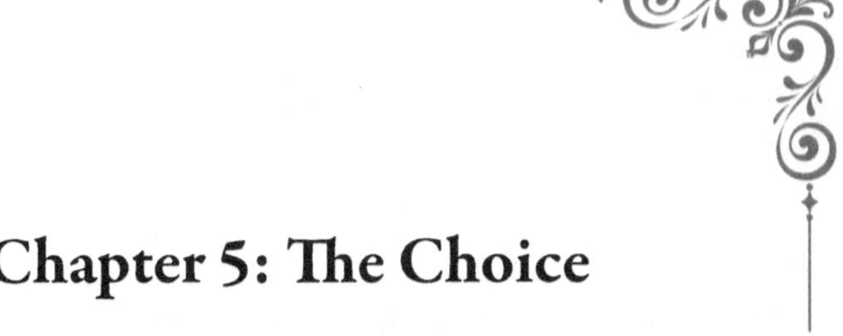

Chapter 5: The Choice

The days after her encounter with the karmic web passed in a blur, each one pulling Amara deeper into a place of reflection. The visions Kael had shown her still haunted her thoughts—the threads, the connections, the choices she had made not just in this life but in many others. For the first time, she began to truly grasp the weight of her existence, and the knowledge both liberated and terrified her.

She could no longer ignore the signs. The whispers, the dreams, the strange coincidences that followed her everywhere—each was a reminder that her life was not as simple as it once seemed. There was a higher purpose calling her, but every step closer to that purpose seemed to reveal how far she had strayed.

Amara tried to immerse herself in her everyday life—work, friends, the comforting routines she had once relied on. But nothing felt the same. The world had shifted around her, and everything she had once known felt foreign. She had outgrown it all, though she wasn't sure where that left her.

It was late one evening when the next shift happened. Amara had been avoiding sleep, fearful of the dreams that had become too real, too urgent. But exhaustion had finally overtaken her, and she drifted off in the early hours of the morning.

This time, the dream wasn't peaceful.

Amara found herself standing at the edge of a vast chasm, the ground beneath her feet crumbling away as dark clouds swirled overhead. The wind howled around her, pulling at her clothes and hair, making it hard to keep her balance. The chasm stretched endlessly in both directions, and on the other side, she could see a faint light—a distant shore that seemed impossibly far away.

She was alone at first, but soon, she felt the familiar presence of Malek behind her.

"You're running out of time, Amara," his voice came, low and filled with a sorrow that chilled her to the bone.

Amara turned to face him. His figure was darker than before, more shadow than man, and the hollow look in his eyes had deepened. The regret that clung to him was palpable, almost suffocating.

"What do you mean?" she asked, though part of her already knew the answer.

"You're standing on the edge," Malek said, stepping closer. "You have to make a choice. Stay where you are, drifting through life, or cross over and face the truth of who you are."

Amara's heart pounded in her chest as she stared at the chasm in front of her. "I don't know how to cross," she said, her voice trembling. "I don't know how to move forward."

Malek's eyes darkened. "If you don't choose, the choice will be made for you."

His words sent a cold shiver down her spine. She could feel the truth in them, the urgency of the moment. The ground beneath her feet trembled, and the edge of the chasm began to crumble, pieces of earth falling away into the darkness below.

Amara stepped back, panic rising in her chest. "What do you want me to do?" she asked, her voice desperate.

Malek's gaze was unreadable. "You have to face yourself. The real you. Not the person you've been pretending to be, not the version of you that hides behind the noise of the world. You have to remember."

Amara's breath came in short gasps as the ground continued to give way beneath her. She felt the pull of the chasm, the dark void below threatening to swallow her whole. The fear of falling, of being lost forever, was overwhelming.

And then, out of the corner of her eye, she saw a flicker of light. Kael.

He stood on the other side of the chasm, his figure glowing softly in the darkness. His eyes met hers, calm and steady, and in that moment, Amara felt a wave of reassurance wash over her.

"You are stronger than your fear, Amara," Kael's voice echoed in her mind. "The path is difficult, but you are not alone."

The wind howled louder, and the gap between where she stood and where Kael waited seemed to widen. Amara's heart raced as she looked from Malek to Kael, unsure of what to do.

"I don't know how to get across," she called to Kael, her voice filled with desperation.

Kael didn't move, but his voice was soft and steady. "The bridge is within you. You've always had the power to cross. You just need to believe it."

Amara looked down at the chasm again. The darkness below seemed endless, a terrifying abyss that beckoned her to fall. But Kael's words echoed in her mind—**"You've always had the power to cross."**

She closed her eyes, trying to calm the panic rising inside her. She had spent so long running from the truth, from the person she was meant to be. The fear of failure, of making the wrong choice, had kept her trapped on the edge, unable to move forward. But now, standing at the brink, she realized that the only thing holding her back was herself.

Taking a deep breath, Amara stepped forward.

The ground shifted beneath her as she moved closer to the edge, but she kept her eyes fixed on Kael. His presence was a beacon of light in the darkness, and she clung to the calm reassurance that radiated from him.

One step. Then another. The edge of the chasm loomed closer, the void below threatening to swallow her, but Amara didn't stop. She could feel the fear clawing at her, trying to pull her back, but she pushed through it.

And then, just as she reached the very edge, she felt something shift inside her. A warmth, a flicker of light that had always been there but had been buried beneath layers of doubt and fear. It was faint at first, but as she focused on it, it grew stronger.

The bridge is within you.

Amara opened her eyes, and to her amazement, she saw a shimmering path appear beneath her feet—a bridge made of light, connecting her side of the chasm to Kael's.

Her heart soared with a mixture of relief and awe as she stepped onto the bridge. The fear that had gripped her moments before faded, replaced by a sense of purpose and determination. She didn't know what lay ahead, but for the first time, she felt ready to face it.

As she crossed the bridge, she glanced back at Malek. He stood at the edge, watching her with an unreadable expression. For a moment, she thought she saw a flicker of something in his eyes—regret, or perhaps longing—but it was gone as quickly as it had appeared.

When Amara reached the other side, Kael was waiting for her. His presence was warm and steady, and as she stood before him, she felt a deep sense of peace settle over her.

"You've made the first step," Kael said softly. "But there is still much work to be done."

Amara nodded, her heart still racing from the intensity of what she had just experienced. "I know," she said, her voice steady. "But I'm ready."

Kael's gaze softened, and he placed a hand on her shoulder. "You've always been ready, Amara. You just had to believe it."

Amara woke with a start, her body covered in a light sheen of sweat. The early morning light filtered through her curtains, casting a soft glow over her room. She lay there for a moment, her mind still reeling from the dream.

But this time, the fear that had been her constant companion was gone. In its place was a sense of clarity, of purpose. She had made her choice. She had crossed the bridge.

Now, it was time to move forward.

The next few days felt different. The heaviness that had been weighing on Amara for weeks had lifted, replaced by a quiet determination. She no longer felt like she was drifting through life, unsure of her place. For the first time, she felt like she was on the right path.

But the journey was far from over.

Amara knew there would be more challenges ahead, more choices to make. But she also knew that she wasn't alone. Kael was with her, guiding her, and the bridge she had crossed was a reminder that she had the strength to face whatever lay ahead.

And Malek... well, she wasn't sure what would become of him. But she hoped, in some way, that he would find his own path. That he would remember who he was.

For now, though, Amara focused on the present. She had made her choice. And that, she realized, was the most powerful step of all.

Chapter 6: The Awakening

The morning after Amara crossed the bridge in her dream, everything felt different.

She awoke with a sense of clarity she hadn't felt in years. The usual heaviness that had clung to her for so long was gone, replaced by a lightness that filled her chest. The world outside her window seemed brighter, sharper, as if she were seeing it for the first time. Even the air felt different—cleaner, clearer, as though she were breathing in something more than just oxygen.

She sat up in bed, staring out at the city skyline, the early morning light casting long shadows across her room. For the first time in weeks, she didn't feel the crushing weight of uncertainty pressing down on her. She didn't feel lost.

But more than that, she felt awake.

It was a strange sensation—this awareness of something greater, something deeper that connected everything around her. She had always sensed that there was more to life than the surface-level reality most people experienced, but now, she could feel it. The energy that pulsed through the world, the unseen forces that shaped everything—it was all around her, and she was part of it.

Her mind raced as she tried to make sense of the shift inside her. The bridge in the dream, Kael's guidance, Malek's warnings—it had all led her to this moment, to this awakening. But what did it mean? What was she supposed to do now?

She got out of bed, her feet touching the cool floor, and walked to the window. The city stretched out before her, bustling with life, people going about their daily routines, unaware of the deeper truths that lay just beneath the surface. Amara watched them, feeling both connected to and separate from the world around her. She was part of this world, but she was no longer bound by it.

The day passed in a blur. At work, Amara moved through her tasks with a calm focus, but her mind was elsewhere. She could feel the shift inside her, the heightened awareness of the energies around her. Conversations with her co-workers seemed distant, almost superficial, as if they were speaking through a veil of illusion. She could hear their words, but the meaning behind them seemed hollow, as though they were going through the motions of their lives without truly living them.

It was unsettling at first, this new perspective. Amara had always felt somewhat out of place in the world, but now that feeling had intensified. She could see the patterns in people's behavior, the unconscious habits and fears that dictated their actions. It was like watching a play unfold, each person following a script they didn't know they had written.

But at the same time, there was a beauty in it. She could see the connections between people, the invisible threads that tied them together. Every action, every word, every thought rippled out into the world, affecting everything around it. She was no longer just a participant in life—she was an observer, a witness to the intricate dance of existence.

By the time the workday ended, Amara was exhausted, not physically, but mentally and emotionally. The heightened awareness was exhilarating, but it was also overwhelming. She had to find a way to balance this new understanding with her everyday life, or she feared she would lose herself in it.

That night, Amara sat on her balcony, the cool evening air washing over her as she stared up at the stars. The city was quiet now, the hustle and bustle of the day giving way to the calm of night. She felt the same stillness inside her, a deep peace that had been elusive for so long.

As she closed her eyes, she felt the presence of Kael. It wasn't as strong as it had been in her dreams, but it was there—a gentle warmth that filled her chest, a quiet whisper in the back of her mind.

"You've taken the first step," Kael's voice echoed softly in her thoughts. "But the journey is far from over."

Amara nodded, her eyes still closed. She knew he was right. Crossing the bridge had been the beginning, but there was still so much she didn't understand.

"What do I do now?" she asked, her voice barely above a whisper.

"Listen," Kael replied. "The answers will come to you in time. But you must stay open. Stay connected."

Amara's brow furrowed. "Connected to what?"

"To yourself," Kael said. "To the truth within you. The world will try to pull you away, to distract you with its noise and illusions. But you must stay grounded in who you are."

Amara opened her eyes, staring up at the night sky. The stars seemed brighter than usual, their light cutting through the darkness. She took a deep breath, letting Kael's words sink in. It was easier said than done, staying connected to herself. The world was full of distractions, full of things that pulled her away from her true path. But she had made it this far. She had crossed the bridge. She could do this.

She had to.

The next few days were a test of Amara's newfound awareness. She could feel the shift inside her, the heightened sensitivity to the energies around her. But with it came new challenges. Every interaction, every conversation seemed to carry a deeper meaning, and it was difficult to separate what was important from what was noise.

At work, she found herself growing more and more disconnected from the routines that had once felt so normal. The meetings, the emails, the deadlines—they all felt trivial now, insignificant compared to the larger truths she had been shown. It was hard to focus on spreadsheets and reports when all she could think about was the karmic web, the unseen forces that shaped every moment of life.

Her co-workers noticed the change, too. Jessica, her friend from the office, had pulled her aside one afternoon.

"Amara, are you okay?" Jessica had asked, her voice full of concern. "You've been so... distant lately."

Amara had forced a smile, trying to brush off the question. "I'm fine, Jess. Just... thinking about a lot of things."

Jessica had frowned but didn't press the issue. "Well, if you need to talk, I'm here, okay?"

Amara had nodded, grateful for her friend's concern, but deep down, she knew that talking wouldn't help. How could she explain what she was going through? How could she tell Jessica about the dreams, the visions, the awakening she was experiencing? It was too much. It would sound insane.

And yet, she knew she couldn't keep it all inside forever.

That evening, Amara returned to the park. It had become a sanctuary for her in recent weeks, a place where she could quiet her mind and connect with the deeper truths she had been shown. The trees stood tall around her, their branches swaying gently in the breeze, and the familiar bench by the pond beckoned her.

She sat down, closing her eyes as the sounds of the city faded into the background. The stillness of the park surrounded her, wrapping her in its comforting embrace.

And then, as she had come to expect, she felt the presence.

"Amara..." The voice was softer than usual, a gentle whisper in the wind. But this time, it wasn't Kael.

It was Malek.

Her heart raced as she opened her eyes, and there he was, standing at the edge of the pond, his dark figure blending into the shadows. His presence was as cold and heavy as it had always been, but there was something different this time—something less threatening, more sorrowful.

"You've changed," Malek said, his voice quiet, almost reverent. "I can see it in you."

Amara stared at him, her emotions a tangled mix of fear and curiosity. "What do you want, Malek?"

Malek's gaze softened, and for the first time, Amara saw a flicker of something in his eyes—regret, or perhaps understanding. "I want you to understand," he said. "I want you to know that what you're doing matters. That you're not just another lost soul, wandering aimlessly through life."

Amara's chest tightened. "I'm not like you," she said, her voice trembling.

Malek shook his head slowly. "No, you're not. You've made the choice I couldn't. You've crossed the bridge. But don't think that your journey is over. You'll be tested. And when you are, you'll need to remember what you've learned."

Amara's pulse quickened. "Tested? What do you mean?"

Malek's expression darkened. "The world will pull you back in, Amara. It will try to make you forget everything you've discovered. The noise, the distractions—they'll be stronger than ever. You have to stay awake. You have to keep moving forward."

Amara's mind raced. She could feel the weight of his words, the truth behind them. But she wasn't sure she was ready for what lay ahead.

"How do I stay awake?" she asked, her voice barely above a whisper.

Malek took a step closer, his presence filling the space between them. "You have to trust yourself," he said. "Trust the guidance you've been given. Trust the light inside you. It's the only thing that will keep you from falling back into the dark."

Amara swallowed hard, her throat tight with emotion. "I'll try," she said, her voice shaking. "But I don't know if I'm strong enough."

Malek's gaze softened, and for the first time, there was a hint of something almost like a smile on his face. "You're stronger than you think," he said softly. "And you're not alone."

As the evening faded into night, Amara walked home with Malek's words echoing in her mind. The tests, the distractions, the noise of the world—they were all waiting for her. But so was the light inside her, the truth she had discovered.

She had awakened, and now it was time to stay awake.

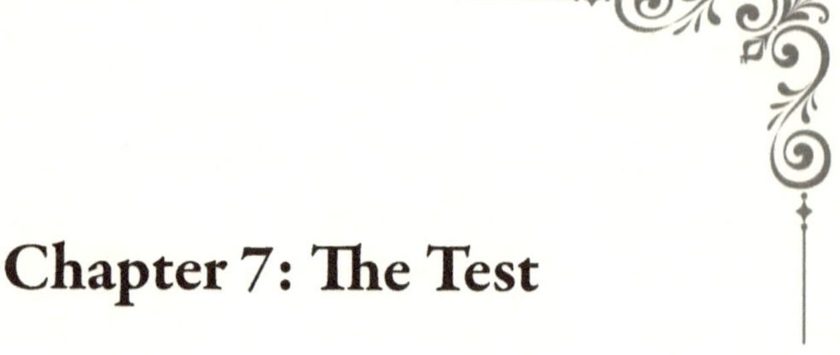

Chapter 7: The Test

The calm Amara had found in the days following her awakening didn't last long. Just as Malek had warned, the world began pulling her back in, and the clarity she had worked so hard to achieve started to blur around the edges.

It began slowly, almost imperceptibly at first. The distractions, the noise of everyday life, crept back into her mind, planting seeds of doubt and confusion. Work had become increasingly stressful—new deadlines, more meetings, more expectations that she found herself struggling to care about. Her friends, too, seemed distant. Conversations that had once been comforting now felt hollow, their words little more than static in the background.

The whispers that had guided her during the early days of her awakening grew quieter, harder to hear amidst the noise. And worst of all, the dreams had stopped. Kael's voice, once a constant presence, had faded into silence, leaving Amara feeling more alone than she had in weeks.

It was a cold Friday morning when Amara first noticed the shift in herself. She had woken up late, her body heavy with exhaustion, her mind clouded by restless sleep. The alarm blared in the background, but it sounded distant, like an annoying hum she couldn't shake off.

She forced herself out of bed, her limbs sluggish as she moved through her morning routine. Her thoughts felt scattered, unfocused, like she was moving through a fog she couldn't seem to break through.

Standing in front of her bathroom mirror, Amara stared at her reflection. She looked the same—her dark hair hanging limply around her face, her eyes dull from lack of sleep—but something felt different. It was as if the person staring back at her wasn't really her, like a version of herself she no longer recognized.

She splashed cold water on her face, hoping to shake off the feeling, but it lingered, gnawing at the edges of her mind.

At work, the day dragged on, each task more tedious than the last. Amara sat in front of her computer, scrolling through emails, but her mind kept wandering. She tried to focus, tried to remind herself of the things that had once felt so clear, but the doubts kept creeping in.

Was any of it real?

The question wormed its way into her thoughts, growing louder with each passing hour. The visions, the dreams, the sense of purpose—it had all felt so vivid, so undeniable at the time. But now, in the cold light of day, surrounded by the monotony of everyday life, it felt distant. Unreal.

By lunch, Amara couldn't take it anymore. She grabbed her coat and left the office, the walls of her cubicle feeling suffocating, the fluorescent lights too harsh. She needed air, space to think.

The city streets were busy, filled with people rushing from one place to another, their faces set in the same tired expressions. Amara weaved through the crowd, her thoughts racing. The sense of clarity she had found in the park, in the dreams, had vanished, replaced by a heavy emptiness that sat in her chest like a stone.

She found herself standing in front of a small café, its windows fogged with warmth from inside. Without thinking, she pushed open the door and stepped inside, the smell of coffee and freshly baked pastries washing over her. It was quieter here, the soft hum of conversation filling the space, but even this felt distant.

Amara ordered a coffee and found a seat by the window, staring out at the street as people hurried by. She watched them, feeling disconnected from the world around her. Everyone seemed so busy, so caught up in their own lives, but it all felt meaningless to her. The conversations, the tasks, the endless cycle of work and sleep and work again—it all felt like noise.

She took a sip of her coffee, her hands trembling slightly. **What's happening to me?** she thought, the question echoing in her mind. She had been so certain of her path just days ago, but now it all felt like it was slipping away.

That night, the dreams returned, but they were different. Gone were the serene fields and the soft, guiding presence of Kael. Instead, Amara found herself standing in a dark forest, the trees looming high above her, their branches twisted and gnarled. The air was thick with fog, and she could barely see a few feet in front of her.

She took a step forward, her foot sinking into the damp earth, and a chill ran down her spine. The forest felt alive, but not in the comforting way she had experienced before. This was different. There was something here—something watching her.

"Amara..." The voice came from behind her, low and cold, and she froze.

She turned slowly, her heart pounding in her chest, and there he was—Malek. He stood a few feet away, his form flickering like a shadow in the mist, his eyes glowing faintly in the darkness.

"You're losing your way," Malek said, his voice quiet but filled with an edge of warning. "The world is pulling you back in."

Amara swallowed hard, her throat tight. "I don't know what to do," she admitted, her voice trembling. "I thought I understood, but now..."

Malek stepped closer, his figure still shrouded in darkness. "You're being tested," he said. "The world will always try to pull you away from the truth. It's easier to fall back into old patterns, to give in to the distractions. But you have to fight it."

Amara's chest tightened with fear. "But how?" she asked, her voice barely above a whisper. "I don't even know if what I experienced was real anymore."

Malek's gaze softened, and for a moment, Amara thought she saw a flicker of something in his eyes—compassion, perhaps, or understanding. "The truth is always real," he said. "But it's up to you to hold onto it."

Amara looked away, her mind racing. She had felt so sure of herself, so certain of her path, but now everything felt uncertain. The noise of the world, the doubts, the fear—they were all closing in on her, clouding her mind.

"You're stronger than this," Malek said, his voice firm. "But you have to choose. The distractions won't stop. The doubts won't go away. But you have the power to push through them. To stay awake."

Amara looked back at him, her eyes filled with uncertainty. "What if I'm not strong enough?"

Malek's expression darkened. "Then you'll end up like me," he said softly, his voice heavy with regret. "Lost. Drifting. A shadow of who you were meant to be."

His words sent a chill down Amara's spine, and she felt a surge of fear rise in her chest. She didn't want to end up like him, trapped in a limbo between the world and the spirit, forever searching for a purpose that could never be fulfilled.

But the fear was paralyzing, and the doubt was louder than ever.

Amara woke with a start, her heart pounding in her chest. The room was dark, the only sound the soft hum of the city outside her window. She sat up, her mind racing, Malek's words echoing in her ears.

You have to choose.

The fear lingered in her chest, but beneath it, she felt something else—resolve. Malek was right. The world would always try to pull her back in, to distract her with its noise and illusions. But she had the power to stay awake, to push through the doubt.

She just had to choose.

The next day, Amara returned to the park. The familiar bench by the pond beckoned her, and she sat down, closing her eyes as the sounds of the city faded into the background. The stillness of the park surrounded her, and for the first time in days, she felt a sense of peace.

She took a deep breath, focusing on the quiet within her. The distractions, the doubts—they were still there, lingering at the edges of her mind, but she didn't let them take over. She let them pass, like clouds drifting across the sky.

And then, in the stillness, she felt it—the presence of Kael. It was faint at first, but it grew stronger, filling her with a warmth that spread through her chest.

"You're not alone," Kael's voice came, soft and reassuring. "You never were."

Amara opened her eyes, her heart swelling with emotion. The world had tried to pull her back in, but she had pushed through. She had made her choice.

She was awake.

Chapter 8: The Whispering Shadows

The days after Amara's test were a strange blur of clarity and confusion. She had pushed through the doubts, chosen to stay awake, but something lingered at the edges of her awareness—something dark and whispering, just beyond her reach. It was as though the more she embraced her spiritual path, the more the shadows of her mind, and perhaps the world, tried to pull her back into the darkness.

She could feel it everywhere. It followed her through the city streets, lingering in the corners of her apartment, clinging to her in moments of silence. It was subtle, almost imperceptible, but it was there—a quiet voice in the back of her mind, a shadowy presence that made her question everything.

One evening, after a particularly long and exhausting day at work, Amara sat at her kitchen table, staring at her notebook. The pages were filled with her scribbled thoughts, dreams, and the lessons she had been learning since her awakening. But tonight, the words seemed distant, like echoes from a time she could no longer grasp.

She flipped through the pages, her fingers brushing over the ink, but something felt off. The sense of purpose, the certainty she had felt after crossing the bridge, had started to slip away again. The noise of the world was creeping back in, and with it came a familiar feeling of unease.

As she stared at the pages, she heard it again—the whisper.

"You're not strong enough."

Amara's breath caught in her throat, her heart skipping a beat. The voice was soft, barely audible, but it sent a chill down her spine. She looked around the room, her eyes scanning the shadows, but there was no one there. Just the empty apartment, silent and still.

"You'll fail."

The whisper came again, more insistent this time. Amara's hands trembled as she closed the notebook, pushing it away from her as if the words on the page had somehow invited the voice. Her chest tightened, a wave of fear washing over her. She had heard whispers before, but they had always been Kael's, guiding her, comforting her. This was different. This was darker.

She stood up from the table, pacing the room as the whispers grew louder in her mind.

"You're not ready."

"You're wasting your time."

Amara shook her head, trying to silence the voice, but it clung to her, wrapping around her thoughts like a suffocating fog. It felt like the shadows themselves were speaking to her, whispering doubts and fears she thought she had already conquered.

She closed her eyes, focusing on her breath, trying to push the voice away. **This isn't real,** she told herself. **This is just my fear talking.**

But the whispers didn't stop.

That night, Amara dreamed of shadows.

She was walking through a dark forest, the same one from her earlier dreams, but this time it was different. The trees were twisted and gnarled, their branches reaching out like skeletal hands, and the air was thick with fog. She could barely see a few feet in front of her, but she knew she wasn't alone.

The shadows followed her, whispering as they moved through the trees. She couldn't see them, but she could feel their presence—cold, heavy, and suffocating. The voices were low and indistinct, like a chorus of whispers carried on the wind.

"Turn back."

"You'll never find your way."

Amara quickened her pace, her heart racing in her chest. The path beneath her feet seemed to stretch on forever, winding deeper and deeper into the dark forest. No matter how fast she walked, the shadows kept pace, their whispers growing louder, more insistent.

"You're not meant for this."

"Give up."

She could feel the fear rising inside her, threatening to overtake her, but she pushed forward. The shadows closed in around her, their voices wrapping around her mind, pulling her into the darkness.

And then, just as she was about to be swallowed by the shadows, she heard a familiar voice—Kael.

"Amara, don't listen."

His voice cut through the darkness like a beam of light, and the shadows seemed to falter for a moment, their whispers fading into the background. Amara stopped, turning in the direction of Kael's voice, but she couldn't see him.

"You're stronger than this," Kael said, his voice calm but firm. **"Don't let the shadows control you."**

Amara took a deep breath, focusing on Kael's words. The shadows were still there, still whispering, but they no longer felt as strong. She could feel their grip loosening, the fog lifting just slightly.

"I don't know what to do," Amara said, her voice trembling. "They won't stop."

"You don't have to fight them," Kael replied. **"You just have to let them pass. They are not part of you. They are illusions, born from fear. Let them go."**

Amara closed her eyes, centering herself in the stillness Kael's presence brought. She took another deep breath, allowing the fear and doubt to wash over her without resisting. She didn't push them away, but she didn't hold onto them either. She simply let them pass, like leaves carried by the wind.

And slowly, the shadows began to fade.

Amara woke with a start, her body drenched in sweat. The room was dark, but the oppressive weight of the shadows from her dream had lifted. She sat up in bed, her heart still racing, but the fear had subsided.

Kael's words echoed in her mind: **"You don't have to fight them. Let them go."**

It was a lesson she hadn't expected but one she knew she needed to learn. The shadows, the whispers—they were not part of her. They were illusions, born from the fear that still lingered in the deepest parts of her mind. And just like the doubts she had faced before, they only had power if she gave it to them.

She took a deep breath, calming herself. The test wasn't over. The world, the shadows, the fear—they would all continue to challenge her. But she didn't have to fight every battle. Sometimes, all she had to do was let go.

The following day, Amara returned to the park. The trees swayed gently in the breeze, their branches casting dappled shadows on the ground. But the shadows here didn't scare her anymore. She had faced them in her dream, and now, in the light of day, they seemed harmless—just shadows, nothing more.

She sat on the bench by the pond, closing her eyes as she let the sounds of the park surround her. The whispers were gone, replaced by the peaceful stillness she had come to cherish. But as she sat there, she couldn't shake the feeling that something deeper was happening—that the shadows she had faced in her dream weren't just figments of her imagination.

There was a darkness in the world, a force that didn't want her to awaken fully. It wasn't just her own doubts and fears that she had to contend with—there were external forces, unseen and whispering, that sought to keep her asleep, to pull her back into the noise and illusions of the world.

Amara opened her eyes, her gaze drifting over the pond's still surface. She knew now that her journey was about more than just personal growth. There was something larger at play, something that wanted to stop her from realizing her full potential.

But she wasn't afraid anymore. She had faced the shadows, and she had come out the other side.

That night, as Amara lay in bed, she felt a deep sense of peace settle over her. The world outside was still full of noise, full of distractions and illusions, but she was no longer at their mercy. She had learned to let go, to trust in herself, and to listen to the whispers of the spirit world instead of the whispers of fear.

The shadows would always be there, lurking at the edges of her awareness. But now, she knew that they had no power over her unless she gave it to them.

She was awake, and she wasn't going back to sleep.

Chapter 9: The Unseen Path

Amara stood at the edge of the park, staring out at the winding path before her. The early morning light filtered through the trees, casting long shadows on the ground, but she wasn't afraid of the shadows anymore. She had faced them, learned to let them pass, and now they were nothing more than fleeting moments of darkness, powerless to pull her back.

But something about today felt different.

There was a weight in the air, a subtle shift that made the world feel more alive, more connected. Amara could feel it in her chest—a gentle pull, like a thread guiding her forward. It was the same feeling she had felt after crossing the bridge in her dream, the sense that something larger than herself was at work, drawing her toward a purpose she was only beginning to understand.

She took a deep breath and started walking, her steps slow and measured. The familiar sounds of the city faded into the background as she moved deeper into the park, her focus narrowing to the path in front of her. The trees seemed taller today, their branches reaching out like arms, guiding her along the way.

For weeks, Amara had been struggling to make sense of everything—the visions, the dreams, the lessons she had learned. But now, there was a sense of clarity settling over her. The doubts, the distractions, even the shadows had lost their grip. She could feel the connection to the spirit world growing stronger, and with it, the awareness that her life was not her own. It was part of something bigger, something unseen.

The path led Amara to the far end of the park, to a small, secluded area she had never noticed before. It was quiet here, the sounds of the city barely reaching this part of the park. The air was cool, and the scent of pine filled her lungs as she breathed deeply, letting the peace of the moment wash over her.

She found a bench nestled under an old oak tree, its branches thick with leaves that swayed gently in the breeze. Sitting down, Amara closed her eyes and let herself sink into the stillness. She had learned that the answers she sought didn't come from outside herself—they came from within. All she had to do was listen.

For a long moment, there was nothing but silence. And then, slowly, she felt it—the presence of Kael.

His warmth filled the space around her, soft and reassuring, like the touch of sunlight on her skin. Amara didn't open her eyes, but she could sense him standing nearby, watching over her as he always did.

"You're beginning to see it," Kael's voice echoed in her mind, calm and steady. "The path you're on is not just your own."

Amara nodded, her eyes still closed. "I can feel it," she said softly. "But I don't know where it's leading."

Kael was silent for a moment, as though weighing his next words. "The path is always unseen, Amara. You won't always know where it's leading, but you must trust that it's taking you exactly where you need to go."

Amara's brow furrowed slightly. She had spent so much of her life searching for control, for certainty, but now she was being asked to trust something she couldn't see, something she didn't fully understand.

"I don't know if I'm ready," she admitted, her voice barely above a whisper. "What if I make the wrong choices?"

Kael's presence was unwavering, a steady light in the darkness. "There are no wrong choices," he said gently. "Every step you take is part of the journey. Even when you think you've strayed from the path, you're still learning, still growing. The important thing is to keep moving forward."

Amara opened her eyes, her gaze drifting over the quiet park. The path in front of her was shrouded in shadow, but she knew now that the shadows weren't something to fear. They were part of the journey, part of the lessons she needed to learn.

"But why me?" she asked, her voice trembling slightly. "Why am I on this path? What is my purpose?"

Kael's voice was soft, but filled with an ancient wisdom that made Amara feel small and infinite all at once. "You have always been on this path, Amara. From the moment your soul was born, you've been walking it. Each life, each choice, has led you here. You are part of the karmic web, just like everyone else. But your purpose is unique."

Amara's heart raced. "What is it? What am I supposed to do?"

Kael's answer was simple. "Heal."

Amara sat with Kael's words, letting them settle into her mind. Heal. The word felt heavy with meaning, yet she wasn't sure she fully understood it. How was she supposed to heal? Who was she supposed to heal?

As if sensing her confusion, Kael continued. "Healing isn't just about others, Amara. It begins with you. You must heal the wounds within yourself before you can help others."

The weight of his words sank into her. For so long, Amara had focused on finding her purpose, on understanding her role in the world, but she hadn't stopped to think about the pain she carried within herself. The doubts, the fears, the regrets from her past lives and this one—they were all part of the burden she had been carrying, and they were holding her back from fully embracing her path.

"I don't know how," she admitted, her voice small and uncertain.

Kael's presence grew warmer, more comforting. "You've already started. Each step you've taken has been part of your healing. Facing your fears, confronting the shadows, choosing to stay awake—it's all part of the process. Healing takes time, but you are not alone in this."

Amara took a deep breath, feeling a wave of emotion rise in her chest. She had been so focused on looking for answers, on trying to figure out what her purpose was, that she hadn't realized the importance of healing herself first.

"I'm scared," she whispered.

Kael's voice was gentle. "It's okay to be scared. Fear is part of the journey. But you are stronger than you know, and you have everything you need to move forward."

Amara nodded, her heart heavy but filled with a sense of calm. She didn't have all the answers yet, but for the first time, she understood that she didn't need to. The path would reveal itself in time. All she had to do was keep walking.

The rest of the day passed in a peaceful blur. Amara returned to her apartment, feeling lighter than she had in weeks. The weight of the world seemed to have lifted, replaced by a quiet sense of purpose that simmered beneath the surface.

She spent the afternoon reading, writing in her notebook, and reflecting on Kael's words. **Heal.** It was such a simple word, yet it held so much meaning. The more she thought about it, the more she realized that healing wasn't just about fixing what was broken. It was about growth, about learning to let go of the things that no longer served her, and about embracing the parts of herself she had been afraid to face.

As the sun began to set, casting a warm glow over her apartment, Amara felt a quiet contentment settle over her. For the first time in a long time, she wasn't rushing to find answers. She wasn't chasing after some elusive sense of purpose. She was simply being, allowing herself to exist in the moment, trusting that the path ahead would unfold as it was meant to.

That night, the dreams returned.

Amara found herself standing in the middle of a vast field, the sky above her dark and filled with stars. The grass beneath her feet was soft and cool, swaying gently in the breeze. There was a stillness in the air, a quiet peace that made her feel as though she were standing at the edge of the universe, looking out into infinity.

And then, she saw him—Kael, standing a few feet away, his figure glowing softly in the starlight.

"You're ready," he said, his voice calm and steady.

Amara took a step toward him, her heart racing. "For what?"

Kael smiled, his eyes filled with warmth. "For the next step. You've done the work, Amara. You've faced the shadows, and you've chosen to heal. Now, it's time to step fully into your purpose."

Amara's breath caught in her throat. "But I don't know what that is yet."

Kael's smile widened. "You will. The path is still unseen, but you are walking it. And as you walk, it will reveal itself."

Amara nodded, her chest filled with a mix of fear and excitement. She didn't know what the future held, but for the first time, she wasn't afraid of the unknown. She trusted the path. She trusted herself.

"I'm ready," she said softly, her voice steady.

Kael's gaze softened, and for a moment, the world seemed to hold its breath. "Then let's begin."

Chapter 10: The First Steps

The days after Amara's encounter with Kael were a blur of energy and anticipation. Something had shifted inside her. The quiet sense of purpose that had been building over the past few weeks had solidified into a clear, unwavering focus. For the first time in her life, Amara didn't feel like she was wandering aimlessly. She was walking a path she could not see, but she knew it was there, waiting for her to step fully into it.

Kael's words echoed in her mind. **"You're ready."**

The thought both excited and terrified her. Ready for what? What exactly was she stepping into?

Amara didn't know the full answer yet, but there was one thing she was certain of: healing. That one word had taken root in her soul, and now, it was all she could think about. She could feel the pull to heal not just herself, but others as well. It was as though the threads of the karmic web she had been shown were now calling out to her, guiding her toward the people and situations where she was meant to make a difference.

It started with small signs.

Amara found herself drawn to people in ways she hadn't been before. At work, she noticed when her co-workers were struggling, picking up on the subtle signs of stress and exhaustion that others might miss. She saw the way Jessica's shoulders slumped when she thought no one was looking, the way Tom's eyes flickered with frustration during meetings. It was as though Amara could see through the masks everyone wore, straight to the pain and doubt beneath.

But instead of feeling overwhelmed by it, she felt a deep sense of compassion. She wanted to help, to ease their burdens, even if it was just in small ways. And so, she began to act.

One afternoon, after a particularly grueling meeting, Amara found herself standing outside the conference room with Jessica. Her friend looked worn out, her usual bright energy dimmed by the weight of endless deadlines and demands.

"You okay?" Amara asked, her voice gentle.

Jessica forced a smile, but it didn't reach her eyes. "Yeah, just... tired. It's been a long week."

Amara nodded, but she didn't let the conversation end there. "You know, you don't have to carry all of this by yourself," she said softly. "It's okay to ask for help."

Jessica blinked, clearly surprised by Amara's words. For a moment, she didn't say anything, and Amara wondered if she had overstepped. But then, Jessica let out a long breath, her shoulders sagging.

"Yeah," she said quietly, her voice tinged with relief. "I guess I forget that sometimes."

Amara smiled, a warmth spreading through her chest. It was a small moment, but she could feel the impact it had. She had seen Jessica's pain, acknowledged it, and in doing so, she had lightened her burden, if only a little.

This, Amara realized, was the beginning of her purpose.

As the days passed, Amara continued to notice these moments—small opportunities to heal, to bring light into the lives of others. Whether it was offering a kind word to a co-worker, lending a listening ear to a friend, or simply being present in the moment, she felt the pull to be more than just a passive observer in the lives of those around her.

But the more she stepped into this role, the more she realized that healing others wasn't just about fixing their problems. It was about holding space for them, about allowing them to feel seen and heard. She couldn't take away their pain or solve their struggles, but she could offer support, compassion, and understanding.

One evening, as Amara sat in her apartment, reflecting on the past few weeks, she felt the familiar presence of Kael. It wasn't as strong as it had been in her dreams, but it was there—a quiet warmth that filled the room, wrapping around her like a soft blanket.

"You're beginning to understand," Kael's voice echoed in her mind, gentle and steady.

Amara smiled, her heart swelling with a sense of peace. "I think so," she replied. "But I still don't know what I'm supposed to do. How do I... heal? How do I know if I'm doing it right?"

Kael's presence grew warmer, more reassuring. "Healing isn't about doing. It's about being. You don't need to have all the answers, Amara. You simply need to show up, to be present, and to listen—to yourself and to others. The rest will follow."

Amara nodded, letting his words sink in. She had spent so much of her life trying to figure everything out, to plan and control every step of the way. But now, she was learning to let go, to trust the path, even if she couldn't see where it was leading.

She was learning that healing wasn't about fixing what was broken—it was about bringing light into the darkness.

But as Amara stepped deeper into her purpose, the challenges grew. The world around her didn't stop pulling her in different directions, and the more she opened herself to the energy of others, the more she felt their pain. At times, it was overwhelming. The weight of the world's suffering pressed down on her, making it hard to breathe.

She wanted to help everyone, to ease their burdens, but she knew she couldn't.

One night, as she lay in bed, her mind racing with thoughts of the people in her life—Jessica, Tom, her family, even strangers she passed on the street—she felt a wave of exhaustion wash over her. The more she tried to heal, the more she felt like she was drowning in the emotions of those around her.

"Kael," she whispered into the darkness, her voice trembling. "I don't know if I can do this. It's too much."

For a long moment, there was only silence. And then, Kael's voice came, soft and steady.

"You're not meant to carry the world, Amara. Healing doesn't mean taking on the pain of others. It means holding space for them, allowing them to heal themselves."

Amara closed her eyes, tears prickling at the corners. "But how do I know when to step in? How do I know when I'm doing enough?"

Kael's presence filled the room, a soothing balm to her weary soul. "You don't need to do anything. Simply be present. The rest will reveal itself in time."

Amara let out a shaky breath, her body relaxing into the comfort of Kael's words. She had been trying so hard to do everything, to help everyone, but she was learning that healing wasn't about saving others. It was about showing up, being present, and trusting that the universe would guide her to the places where she was needed most.

The next morning, Amara woke with a renewed sense of purpose. She didn't have all the answers, but she no longer felt the pressure to fix everything. She understood now that her role was to be a light in the darkness, to offer compassion and support, but not to take on the burdens of others as her own.

As she moved through the day, she carried this new awareness with her. The small moments of connection—an encouraging word to a co-worker, a smile to a stranger, a quiet moment of reflection—became acts of healing in themselves. And with each one, Amara felt more grounded in her purpose.

That evening, Amara found herself back at the park, sitting on the familiar bench by the pond. The trees swayed gently in the breeze, their branches casting long shadows on the ground. The air was cool and crisp, and the stillness of the park filled her with a sense of peace.

She closed her eyes, letting the sounds of the park surround her, and for a moment, she simply breathed. There were no whispers, no shadows, no doubts—just the quiet stillness of the present moment.

And then, in the silence, she felt it—the connection to the unseen web that tied everything together. The karmic threads that linked her to the people in her life, to the world, to the universe itself. She could feel the pull of those threads, the gentle tug guiding her forward.

You're ready, Kael's voice echoed in her mind, and this time, Amara didn't feel any fear.

She was ready.

Chapter 11: A Shift in the Wind

THE CHANGE CAME QUIETLY at first, like the faint rustling of leaves before a storm. Amara felt it in the subtle shifts of energy around her, in the way the air seemed to hum with something unseen. She had grown attuned to these kinds of feelings, but this was different. It wasn't just the usual signs she had come to recognize. This felt like a warning, a signal that something important was on the horizon.

For days, the sense of impending change lingered in the back of her mind, casting a shadow over everything she did. At work, she found herself distracted, her thoughts drifting toward the strange dreams that had returned. They were different now—more vivid, more urgent. In these dreams, she stood on the edge of something vast and unknowable, with winds swirling around her and voices calling her name.

"You're not ready," the voices whispered. "You're not strong enough."

But there was another voice, calm and steady, that cut through the fear. **Kael's.**

"You are ready," he said softly. "But the path ahead is difficult. You must stay grounded."

Amara woke from these dreams feeling both energized and unnerved. She didn't know what was coming, but she could feel it getting closer with each passing day.

One afternoon, after another long day at the office, Amara decided to take a walk to clear her mind. The park had become her sanctuary, a place where she could connect with herself and the spirit world in peace. But today, even the familiar comfort of the trees and the pond couldn't shake the feeling that something was shifting.

As she walked along the path, her thoughts swirling with questions, she saw something—or rather, someone—that stopped her in her tracks.

A man stood near the edge of the pond, staring out at the water. There was something about him that felt familiar, though Amara was sure she had never seen him before. He was tall, with dark hair that curled slightly at the ends, and his presence seemed to hum with an energy that made the air around him feel charged.

Amara's heart raced as she approached him, the sense of recognition growing stronger with each step. She didn't know why, but she felt drawn to him, as though some invisible force was pulling her closer.

The man turned as she neared, his eyes locking onto hers with an intensity that sent a shiver down her spine. For a moment, neither of them spoke. Then, he smiled—a slow, knowing smile that made Amara feel as though he understood something she hadn't yet grasped.

"You've felt it, haven't you?" he said, his voice low and steady.

Amara blinked, caught off guard. "Felt what?"

"The shift," he said simply. "The change that's coming. It's why you're here."

Amara's breath caught in her throat. "How do you know that?"

The man's smile widened, but there was no malice in it—only understanding. "Because I've felt it too."

They talked for what felt like hours, sitting by the pond as the sun dipped lower in the sky. The man's name was Ethan, and like Amara, he had been on a spiritual journey for most of his life. He spoke of signs, of dreams, of a sense that the world was on the verge of something big—something that required people like them to step into their purpose.

"There are more of us out there than you think," Ethan said, his eyes fixed on the horizon. "People who are waking up, who are realizing that we're all connected—that we're part of something larger. But not everyone knows what to do with that knowledge. That's why we need to find each other."

Amara listened, her heart racing. It was as though Ethan was speaking directly to the thoughts she had been grappling with for weeks. The pull she had felt, the sense that her purpose was tied to something greater—it wasn't just in her head. It was real, and it was happening to others too.

"You're not alone," Ethan said, turning to look at her. "None of us are. But we have to find each other if we're going to be ready for what's coming."

Amara nodded, her mind spinning. She had spent so much of her journey feeling isolated, unsure of how to move forward. But now, sitting here with Ethan, she realized that she wasn't alone in this. There were others like her—others who had felt the call, who were searching for their place in the world.

And together, they were stronger.

As the sky darkened and the first stars appeared, Amara and Ethan said their goodbyes, promising to meet again soon. But as she made her way home, a new sense of determination settled over her.

There was something coming—something bigger than she had imagined. And for the first time, she wasn't afraid. She was ready to face whatever lay ahead, knowing that she wasn't walking this path alone.

Chapter 12: The Circle Gathers

A week passed, and the pull grew stronger. Amara had been meeting with Ethan regularly, sharing their experiences and deepening their understanding of the spiritual shifts happening around them. With each conversation, Amara felt herself growing more certain of her purpose, more aligned with the path she had been called to walk.

But it wasn't just Ethan. In the days following their first meeting, Amara began to notice others—people who seemed to carry the same quiet energy, the same sense of knowing. It was subtle at first, just a feeling she couldn't quite explain. But as time went on, the connections became more obvious.

She started seeing the same people at the park, on the streets, even at work—people who looked at her with a kind of recognition, as though they knew exactly what she was going through. Some of them smiled, others simply nodded, but the message was clear: she wasn't alone.

And then came the invitation.

It arrived one afternoon, slipped under the door of her apartment. A plain envelope, unmarked except for her name written in neat, elegant handwriting. Inside was a single card, printed with a simple message:

"You are not alone. The circle gathers. Join us."

Beneath the words was an address and a time—tonight, at 7 PM.

Amara stared at the card, her heart racing. This was it. The circle Ethan had spoken of. The people who were waking up, who were beginning to understand their place in the karmic web. She didn't know what to expect, but she knew she had to go.

That evening, as the sun dipped below the horizon, Amara found herself standing outside an old building tucked away on a quiet street. The windows were dark, and the only light came from a single lantern hanging above the door, casting a soft glow over the entrance.

Her heart pounded as she approached the door, her fingers trembling slightly as she reached for the handle. For a moment, she hesitated. What if this was all a mistake? What if she was walking into something she wasn't ready for?

But then, Kael's voice echoed in her mind. **"You are ready."**

Taking a deep breath, Amara pushed open the door and stepped inside.

The room was dimly lit, the soft flicker of candles casting shadows on the walls. A small group of people sat in a circle in the center of the room, their faces illuminated by the warm glow of the flames. As Amara entered, all eyes turned to her, but there was no judgment, no hesitation—only welcome.

Ethan was there, sitting near the back of the circle, and he smiled as she walked toward him, motioning for her to join them.

"We've been waiting for you," he said softly as she sat down beside him.

Amara glanced around the room, taking in the faces of the people gathered there. Some were young, others older, but they all shared the same quiet energy, the same sense of purpose that she had felt growing inside herself.

"We're all here for the same reason," Ethan said, his voice calm and steady. "We've all felt the call. And now, we're beginning to understand what it means."

The room fell silent as a woman at the center of the circle stood, her presence commanding yet gentle. She was older, her silver hair pulled back in a loose bun, and her eyes glowed with a wisdom that made Amara feel both comforted and awed.

"My name is Liora," the woman said, her voice resonating through the room. "And like you, I have felt the shift. The world is changing, and we are being called to step into our purpose. Each of us has a role to play in what is coming, and together, we can help heal the wounds of this world."

Amara's breath caught in her throat. This was it. This was what she had been searching for—her place in the larger web of existence, her connection to something greater than herself.

As Liora continued to speak, Amara felt a deep sense of peace settle over her. She wasn't just a passive participant in this journey anymore. She was part of something much bigger, something that had the power to change the world.

And for the first time, she understood what Kael had meant when he told her she was ready.

She was ready to step into her purpose. Ready to heal—not just herself, but the world around her.

Chapter 13: The Call to Action

The days after the circle gathering passed in a blur of activity. Amara felt more alive than she had in years, her mind buzzing with the energy of the people she had met, the conversations they had shared. For the first time, she felt like she was part of a community—one that understood her, one that was walking the same path she was.

But with that sense of belonging came a new responsibility. Amara knew she couldn't simply sit back and observe anymore. It was time to take action, to step fully into the role she had been preparing for all along.

The first test came sooner than she expected.

It was a Wednesday afternoon, and Amara was sitting at her desk, finishing up some paperwork before a meeting, when her phone buzzed with a text message. She glanced at the screen, expecting it to be one of her friends, but her heart skipped a beat when she saw the name.

It was her brother, Liam.

"Hey, can we talk? It's important."

Amara frowned, her stomach twisting with a sudden sense of dread. She and Liam had never been particularly close. They had grown up in the same house, but their lives had taken different paths. While Amara had always been drawn to the spiritual, to the unseen forces that shaped the world, Liam had stayed firmly grounded in the material, focused on his career and his family.

But something about the message made Amara's heart race. She could feel the urgency behind his words, the unspoken plea for help.

Without thinking, she grabbed her phone and stepped outside, dialing his number as she walked toward the park. The phone rang twice before Liam picked up, his voice tight with emotion.

"Amara," he said, and she could hear the strain in his voice. "I need your help."

They met later that evening at a small café near Liam's office. Amara hadn't seen him in months, and the first thing she noticed was how tired he looked. His usual confident demeanor was gone, replaced by a weariness that made him seem smaller somehow.

"What's going on?" Amara asked, her voice soft but filled with concern.

Liam sighed, running a hand through his hair. "It's... everything. Work, the kids, the house. It's all falling apart, and I don't know how to fix it."

Amara's heart ached for him. She could see the weight of the world pressing down on him, the same weight she had felt not long ago. But she also knew that this wasn't something she could fix for him. He had to find his own way through it.

"Liam," she said gently, reaching across the table to take his hand. "You don't have to do this alone. But you also don't have to carry all of it by yourself."

He looked at her, his eyes filled with a mix of frustration and exhaustion. "I don't know how to let go," he admitted, his voice cracking. "I've always been the one who fixes things. But now... now I feel like I'm drowning."

Amara squeezed his hand, her heart breaking for him. "You're not drowning," she said softly. "You're just lost. And that's okay. We all get lost sometimes."

For a long moment, they sat in silence, the weight of Liam's struggles hanging heavy in the air. But Amara could feel the shift happening—the slow realization dawning on her brother that he didn't have to do this alone.

"Let's take it one step at a time," Amara said finally. "You don't have to have all the answers right now. But you do need to take care of yourself. You can't help anyone else if you're falling apart."

Liam nodded, his eyes glistening with unshed tears. "I just don't know where to start."

Amara smiled, a soft, reassuring smile that she hoped would ease some of his burden. "Start by letting go of the need to control everything. Trust that things will work out, even if you can't see how right now."

That night, as Amara walked home, she felt the weight of the conversation with Liam settle over her. She had always known that part of her purpose was to help others heal, but this felt different. This was her family—her brother—and for the first time, she understood that healing wasn't just about strangers or distant acquaintances. It was about the people closest to her, too.

She had stepped into her purpose, but the path ahead was still full of challenges. There would be more conversations like the one with Liam, more moments where she would have to hold space for others, even when it felt overwhelming.

But Amara knew now that she was ready. She had been preparing for this her entire life.

Chapter 14: Facing the Dark

The next few weeks passed in a whirlwind of activity. Amara continued to meet with the circle, deepening her connection with the people who had become like family to her. Together, they shared their experiences, supported one another, and explored the spiritual shifts happening around them.

But even as Amara grew more confident in her role as a healer, she couldn't shake the feeling that something darker was looming on the horizon.

It started with the dreams.

At first, they were nothing more than fleeting images—shadows moving through the trees, whispers in the dark. But as the days passed, the dreams became more vivid, more intense. Amara found herself standing on the edge of a great void, with winds howling around her and voices calling her name.

"You're not ready," the voices whispered. **"You're not strong enough."**

The dreams left her shaken, her mind racing with questions she couldn't answer. Was this another test? Or was something darker at play—something that wanted to pull her back into the shadows she had worked so hard to escape?

One night, as Amara lay in bed, the dreams returned, more powerful than ever. She stood in the middle of a dark forest, the trees twisted and gnarled, their branches reaching out like skeletal hands. The air was thick with fog, and she could barely see a few feet in front of her.

But this time, she wasn't alone.

Malek stood before her, his form flickering like a shadow in the mist, his eyes glowing faintly in the darkness.

"You're losing your way," he said, his voice low and cold. "The world is pulling you back in."

Amara's heart raced, fear tightening in her chest. "What do you mean?"

Malek stepped closer, his presence oppressive and heavy. "You think you're strong enough to face what's coming. But you're not. You're still clinging to the illusions of this world—the need to be in control, the fear of letting go. And that's what will destroy you."

Amara shook her head, her voice trembling. "No. I've let go. I'm ready."

Malek's lips curled into a bitter smile. "You think you're ready because you've seen the light. But you haven't faced the darkness—not fully. And until you do, you'll never be free."

Amara woke with a start, her body drenched in sweat, her heart pounding in her chest. The room was dark, the only sound the soft hum of the city outside her window. But the weight of Malek's words pressed down on her, filling her with a sense of dread she couldn't shake.

Was he right? Had she only scratched the surface of her spiritual awakening? Had she been so focused on the light that she had ignored the darkness lurking within herself?

She didn't know the answers, but one thing was clear: the path ahead was far more difficult than she had imagined.

And now, it was time to face the darkness.

Chapter 15: The Descent

The days after her encounter with Malek were the hardest Amara had faced since her awakening. The darkness he had spoken of—the part of herself she hadn't fully confronted—loomed larger and more ominous. Every day, she could feel its presence more acutely, like a shadow that followed her wherever she went. She had hoped that facing the light and choosing to heal would be enough. But now, she realized that the journey wasn't complete until she faced the darkness within herself.

For the first time in weeks, Amara didn't feel ready. The confidence she had gained, the peace she had found in her purpose, all seemed to unravel as she came face to face with her doubts. Kael's presence, once a constant source of comfort, felt more distant now. He was still there, but he had grown quieter, as if urging her to find her own strength.

It was a chilly evening when the final confrontation with her own darkness began. Amara had been sitting in the circle with the others, but something felt different this time. The usual warmth and connection between them was replaced by an uncomfortable tension that clung to the air. Liora, always calm and composed, had a look of concern on her face as she spoke to the group.

"There is a shift coming," she said, her voice quiet but firm. "A moment where each of us will have to face what we've been avoiding. You've all made incredible progress on your spiritual journeys, but this is only the beginning. The real work begins when you confront the parts of yourself you're most afraid to see."

Amara's heart tightened in her chest. She had known this was coming. Malek's warnings had been clear, but hearing Liora confirm it filled her with a sense of dread. She had worked so hard to reach this point, but now, it felt as though all of her progress was slipping away.

After the circle dispersed, Amara lingered, her mind swirling with thoughts. Ethan noticed her hesitation and walked over, his brow furrowed with concern.

"You okay?" he asked softly, sitting down beside her.

Amara shook her head, her eyes distant. "No. I don't think I am."

Ethan studied her for a moment, his expression thoughtful. "You're worried about what's coming, aren't you?"

She nodded, a lump forming in her throat. "I feel like I'm losing everything I've worked for. Like I'm about to be pulled back into something dark."

Ethan was silent for a moment before he spoke. "You're not losing anything, Amara. You're just going deeper. The darkness you're feeling—it's part of you. But it's not something to be afraid of. It's something you have to face."

Amara looked at him, her eyes filled with uncertainty. "But what if I'm not strong enough?"

Ethan smiled, his voice gentle. "You are. We all are. But you won't know that until you walk through the fear."

That night, Amara lay awake in bed, staring at the ceiling. The conversation with Ethan had left her with more questions than answers. She didn't know how to confront the darkness, didn't even know where to begin. But she knew she couldn't avoid it any longer.

The dreams came again—stronger, darker, more vivid than ever before.

Amara stood in the middle of the dark forest, the trees twisted and gnarled like they had been in her previous dreams. But this time, the shadows were thicker, the air heavier with a sense of dread. She could hear the whispers all around her, soft and insidious, filling her mind with doubt.

"You're not ready."

"You're not strong enough."

The words echoed through the trees, but this time, Amara didn't run. She stood her ground, her heart pounding in her chest, and faced the darkness head-on.

Out of the shadows, Malek appeared, his form flickering like a dying flame. His eyes glowed faintly in the darkness, and his expression was unreadable as he approached her.

"You've come to face it," Malek said softly, his voice a low murmur that sent chills down Amara's spine. "But are you ready to see what lies within?"

Amara swallowed hard, her throat dry. "I don't know," she admitted. "But I can't keep running."

Malek's lips curled into a faint, sad smile. "No, you can't. The darkness is part of you, Amara. You can't heal fully until you accept that."

The shadows around them seemed to thicken, the darkness pressing in closer as if it was alive, pulsating with the energy of her deepest fears. Amara's heart raced, but she forced herself to breathe, to stay present in the moment.

"What do I need to do?" she asked, her voice trembling.

Malek stepped closer, his figure almost merging with the shadows around him. "You need to face what you've been hiding from. Your pain. Your fears. The parts of yourself you've buried because they were too hard to look at. The light is only half of the journey. The other half is in the dark."

Amara closed her eyes, her breath coming in shallow gasps as the weight of Malek's words sank in. She had spent so much time focusing on healing, on finding the light, that she hadn't realized she was avoiding the darkness within herself. But now, she could feel it—every regret, every doubt, every moment of pain she had ever experienced, bubbling up to the surface.

Her body trembled as the shadows closed in around her, but she didn't run. She couldn't. Not anymore.

She took a deep breath, her hands clenching into fists at her sides. "I'm ready," she whispered.

And with that, the darkness swallowed her whole.

Amara was plunged into the depths of her own mind, her consciousness spiraling through memories and emotions she had long buried. She saw herself as a child, alone in her room, crying because she didn't understand why she felt different from everyone else. She saw herself as a teenager, struggling to fit in, to be what everyone expected her to be. And she saw herself as an adult, pretending to have it all together while quietly breaking apart inside.

Each memory, each moment of pain, hit her like a tidal wave, overwhelming her senses. She could feel the weight of it pressing down on her, the fear that she had carried for so long threatening to drown her.

But then, in the midst of the darkness, she heard a voice—a soft, steady whisper that cut through the chaos.

"You are not your pain."

It was Kael. His presence was faint, but it was there, like a beacon of light in the darkness. Amara clung to his words, her breath coming in ragged gasps as she fought to hold on to herself.

"You are not your fear. You are more than the darkness."

The words wrapped around her like a lifeline, pulling her out of the depths of her despair. Slowly, the shadows began to recede, the weight of the darkness lifting as Kael's presence grew stronger.

Amara opened her eyes, and for the first time, she could see clearly. The darkness hadn't been something outside of her—it had been within her all along. But now, standing in the middle of it, she realized it didn't have to control her.

She was stronger than the darkness. She always had been.

When Amara woke the next morning, the weight of the dream still clung to her, but she felt different. Lighter. More whole. The darkness was still there, but now she understood that it wasn't something to fear. It was part of her, but it didn't define her.

For the first time, she had faced her deepest fears and come out the other side. And she knew, deep in her soul, that this was the true beginning of her journey.

Chapter 16: The Rising

Amara had faced the darkness, but the journey wasn't over. If anything, she realized that confronting her fears was only the beginning of something much deeper. The relief she had felt after waking from the dream of shadows was short-lived. With each passing day, the world around her seemed to grow heavier, filled with challenges she hadn't anticipated.

Yet, despite the weight of everything, there was also a quiet strength building inside her—a strength she hadn't felt before. The dark forest had not broken her. It had made her stronger, more aware of her own power.

She wasn't afraid anymore.

Days passed, and Amara threw herself back into her spiritual work with a renewed sense of purpose. The gatherings with Ethan and the others in the circle became more frequent, and each time they met, Amara could feel their collective energy growing. There was something powerful about being surrounded by people who understood what she was going through—people who had faced their own darkness and were learning how to heal.

But even as they shared their stories and offered support to one another, there was a growing sense that something big was coming. A shift, a turning point that would change everything.

"We're being called to act," Liora said one evening as the group gathered in the small, candlelit room. "The world around us is changing, and we're being called to step into our roles as healers, as guides. But we cannot do this work alone. We must support one another."

Amara listened, her heart beating steadily in her chest. She had known this moment was coming, but hearing Liora speak the words out loud made it feel more real. The path ahead was no longer just about personal healing—it was about helping others. About stepping fully into her purpose and accepting the responsibility that came with it.

But what exactly was that responsibility? Amara still wasn't sure. She had healed herself, but now she had to learn how to extend that healing outward, to the people and the world around her. And with that realization came a new fear: What if she wasn't enough? What if she couldn't help the people who needed her?

That night, after the meeting, Amara stayed behind to talk with Liora. There was something about the older woman that radiated wisdom and calm, and Amara found herself seeking her guidance more and more.

"I feel like something is happening," Amara said softly as they sat together in the dimly lit room. "Like we're being prepared for something bigger. But I don't know if I'm ready."

Liora smiled gently, her eyes filled with understanding. "None of us ever feel ready when the time comes. But you've already taken the first step, Amara. You've faced your darkness, and you've come through the other side. That's more than most people ever do."

Amara frowned, her hands twisting in her lap. "But what if I can't do it? What if I'm not enough?"

Liora reached out, placing a hand on Amara's shoulder. "You are enough, exactly as you are. But the strength you need doesn't come from trying to control the outcome. It comes from letting go, from trusting that you are being guided."

Amara nodded, though the doubt still lingered at the edges of her mind. "It's hard to let go," she admitted.

Liora's smile softened. "I know. But that's the key, Amara. The power you're looking for is already within you. You just need to trust it."

The next morning, Amara woke to a sense of calm she hadn't felt in a long time. The weight of the past few days was still there, but it no longer felt as heavy. She had faced the darkness, and now it was time to rise.

She spent the day reflecting on the lessons she had learned, writing in her notebook, and meditating in the park. The trees, the breeze, the sound of birds—it all felt different now, more alive, more connected. She could feel the energy of the world around her, the unseen threads that tied everything together.

But there was also a sense of urgency. Something was shifting, not just within her, but in the world itself.

As she sat on the familiar bench by the pond, her eyes closed in quiet meditation, she felt a presence beside her. She didn't need to open her eyes to know it was Kael.

"You've grown," his voice came, soft and steady. "You're beginning to understand."

Amara smiled, her heart filling with warmth at the sound of his voice. "I think I am. But I still don't know what comes next."

Kael was silent for a moment, his presence strong but gentle. "What comes next isn't something you can control. The world is changing, and you're part of that change. But you can't force it. You can only trust in the process."

Amara nodded, letting his words sink in. She had spent so much of her life trying to control everything—her emotions, her path, the outcomes of every situation. But now, she was learning to let go, to trust that she didn't need all the answers.

The shift came a few days later, when Amara least expected it.

She was at work, going through her usual tasks, when she received a message from Ethan. **"We need to meet tonight. Something's happening."**

The urgency in his words made Amara's pulse quicken. She didn't know what he meant, but she could feel it too—something was shifting. The air around her felt charged, like the moments before a storm. Without hesitation, she replied to Ethan's message, agreeing to meet him at the park after work.

As she walked toward the park that evening, her heart raced with a mix of anticipation and fear. She could feel the energy building, the pull toward something she couldn't yet see but knew was coming.

When she arrived, Ethan was already there, standing by the pond with a group of others from the circle. They all had the same look of quiet determination on their faces, as if they knew that whatever was coming, it was big.

"What's going on?" Amara asked as she approached.

Ethan turned to her, his expression serious. "There's been a disturbance. Something's changed in the energy, and we need to figure out what it means."

Amara frowned, her mind racing. "What kind of disturbance?"

"We don't know yet," Ethan admitted. "But we can all feel it. The energy has shifted, and it's affecting more than just us. We need to come together, to figure out what we're supposed to do."

Amara nodded, a sense of calm washing over her. This was it. The shift they had been preparing for. The moment when they would need to step fully into their roles as healers, as guides.

As the group gathered in a circle, holding hands and closing their eyes, Amara felt the energy around them grow stronger. The wind picked up, swirling around them, and she could feel the connection between each person, the threads of energy that linked them together.

For a long time, they sat in silence, allowing the energy to move through them, to guide them. And then, slowly, Amara began to feel it—a new presence. Not just Kael, but something larger, something more powerful than she had ever felt before.

The presence filled her with warmth, with light, and with a deep sense of purpose. It was as though the universe itself was speaking to her, telling her that this was her moment. This was what she had been preparing for all along.

When she opened her eyes, she knew. The rising had begun.

Chapter 17: The Unveiling

The energy in the circle felt electrified, alive with a force that none of them could deny. As Amara sat among the group by the pond, she could feel the hum of something powerful, something ancient moving through her. It was as if the very air around them was charged with a purpose that went beyond anything they had experienced before. For so long, they had been preparing, healing, waiting. Now, it felt like the moment had arrived.

As they sat in meditation, eyes closed, hands linked, Amara's mind drifted into a state of stillness. The world around her seemed to fall away, leaving only the steady beat of her heart and the gentle rhythm of her breath. She could feel Kael's presence beside her, and for the first time in days, the calm assurance of his energy soothed her worries.

But something else was there too—something bigger.

It started as a soft vibration, a subtle shift in the air, but soon it grew. The energy swirled around them like a current, pulling them deeper into a collective consciousness. Amara's heart raced as she sensed the presence of something powerful—a force that connected them all, weaving through them like an unseen thread.

And then, she saw it.

A vision bloomed before her eyes. She was no longer sitting in the park; instead, she stood on the edge of a vast landscape, staring out at a world that seemed to shimmer with light. The colors were more vibrant, the air filled with a sense of clarity and peace that took her breath away.

This place wasn't familiar, yet it felt like home.

As she looked around, she saw others—people she knew, people she didn't—all standing together, connected by the same force. They were scattered across the landscape, but each of them radiated light, their presence filled with a sense of purpose. Amara felt the weight of this moment settle over her. This was the unveiling—the moment when everything they had been preparing for would be revealed.

She took a step forward, her feet sinking into the soft, glowing earth, and felt a pull deep within her. The vision expanded, showing her glimpses of the past, the present, and the future all at once. She saw herself struggling as a kid, feeling the weight of the world even then. She saw her struggles, her pain, her journey toward healing. And she saw the darkness she had faced, the shadows that had once threatened to consume her.

But now, she saw something more. She saw the threads of connection between herself and the others, not just in this circle, but across the world. These threads of energy weren't limited by time or space—they reached into the past, into the future, and beyond. Every action, every decision, was part of a larger web that held the universe together.

This is your path. Kael's voice echoed in her mind, strong and clear. **You were never alone. You are part of this. All of you are.**

Amara's heart swelled with emotion. She had known this, but now she could see it, feel it in every fiber of her being. The journey she had been on wasn't just about healing herself—it was about healing the world. And she wasn't the only one. They were all part of this, every person in the circle, and beyond.

The vision shifted again, and this time, she saw the future. The landscape before her was filled with light, but it was also filled with challenges—darkness and light in constant motion, constantly balancing one another. She saw people struggling, hurting, lost. But she also saw healing. She saw hands reaching out to help, saw the power of love and connection, saw how one small act of kindness could ripple across the entire web, touching lives she couldn't even imagine.

And she saw her role in it all.

When Amara's eyes fluttered open, she was back in the park, the group around her still locked in meditation. The night was cool, and the wind whispered softly through the trees. But the energy was still there, still vibrating through her, connecting them all.

She looked around at the faces of the people she had come to trust—Ethan, Liora, and the others. They were all part of this, part of the same unveiling. She could see it in their eyes, the same recognition, the same knowing. They had seen it too.

"We're not alone," Amara whispered, her voice barely audible. But Ethan heard her, and he nodded, his eyes filled with the same wonder she felt.

"No," he said softly. "We're not."

For the rest of the evening, they sat in silence, letting the energy of the moment settle over them. No one spoke, but there was no need. They had all felt the shift. They had all seen what was coming.

When they finally stood to leave, Amara felt lighter than she had in weeks. The fear that had once gripped her was gone, replaced by a quiet certainty. She didn't know all the details, didn't have all the answers, but she knew enough.

They were part of something much larger than themselves. And whatever was coming, they would face it together.

The next morning, Amara woke with a sense of purpose that she hadn't felt in a long time. The vision from the night before lingered in her mind, vivid and clear. The landscape, the light, the threads of connection—it was all still with her, like a map imprinted on her soul.

But with that clarity came a new urgency. There was still so much work to be done.

As she got ready for the day, she couldn't shake the feeling that something big was about to happen. She had felt the energy building for weeks, but now, it seemed like everything was about to come to a head. The unveiling had shown her the path, but now she had to walk it.

Later that day, she met Ethan for coffee. They had agreed to meet and discuss what they had experienced the night before, but Amara could see the same urgency in his eyes that she felt in her own.

"Something's happening," Ethan said as soon as they sat down. "I don't know what it is yet, but I can feel it."

Amara nodded, her hands wrapped around the warm cup of coffee. "I felt it too. It's like everything we've been working toward is about to unfold."

They sat in silence for a moment, both of them grappling with the weight of the moment. For so long, they had been preparing—healing, learning, growing. But now, it felt like the time for preparation was over.

"Do you think we're ready?" Amara asked quietly.

Ethan didn't answer right away, his gaze thoughtful. "I think we have to be," he said finally. "Whatever's coming, it's bigger than any one of us. But we're not alone. That's what the vision showed me. We're all connected. And together, we're stronger."

Amara smiled, the warmth of his words filling her with a sense of hope. He was right. They weren't alone. They had each other, and they had the strength of the circle. Whatever was coming, they would face it together.

That night, as Amara lay in bed, she felt the familiar presence of Kael beside her. His energy was calm, steady, like a reassuring hand on her shoulder.

"You've seen the path," Kael's voice came softly. "Now it's time to walk it."

Amara closed her eyes, her heart swelling with a mixture of fear and excitement. "What comes next?" she asked.

Kael was silent for a moment, his presence warm and comforting. "The unveiling was just the beginning," he said finally. "The world is changing, Amara. You've seen the light, but there is still darkness to come. You've learned how to heal yourself, but now you must learn how to heal others."

Amara's breath caught in her throat. "How do I do that?"

Kael's voice was soft, but filled with an ancient wisdom. "By being who you are. By trusting in the connection you've felt, the threads that bind you to others. Healing isn't about fixing. It's about holding space, about being present in the lives of those who need you."

Amara nodded, her heart pounding in her chest. She had come so far, but the road ahead was still long. There would be challenges, darkness she hadn't yet faced. But she wasn't afraid anymore.

She had the light within her, and she wasn't walking this path alone.

Chapter 18: The Gathering Storm

The world around Amara seemed to hold its breath. The unveiling had shown her the path, the interconnectedness of all things, but it also hinted at the challenges that lay ahead. She could feel the shift not just in herself but in the world around her. The air seemed heavier, as though it was waiting for something to happen, something that could change everything.

Amara had shared her experience with the circle, and each person had felt something similar. Ethan's words from the previous night echoed in her mind: **"We have to be ready."** The urgency that had been simmering beneath the surface now surged to the forefront. The time for waiting was over.

But what was it that they were waiting for? What was this shift they could all feel but couldn't quite define?

Over the next few days, Amara began to notice subtle changes around her—people in the city seemed more restless, more on edge. Conversations at work were filled with complaints about how strange things felt, how the weather seemed out of sync, how people were losing patience over the smallest things. It was as if everyone could sense something, even if they couldn't name it.

The energy in the air was different—charged, almost electric.

Amara met with Ethan nearly every evening after work, sharing their thoughts and trying to make sense of what was happening. Each time they gathered, the circle members discussed their growing awareness that something was coming. But even with all their collective insight, they couldn't pinpoint exactly what the change would be. The unveiling had shown them the need to be ready, but it hadn't shown them how to prepare.

"I can feel it too," Liora said one evening as they sat together in the candlelit room where they often met. "The world is shifting. We've all felt it. But what we need to remember is that we are part of that shift. We're not just bystanders. We are active participants in this transformation."

Amara looked around at the faces of the group. Each person carried a look of determination, but there was also fear. How could they help change the world when they didn't know what was coming?

Ethan spoke up, his voice steady but serious. "We need to trust what we've learned, trust our instincts. Whatever happens, we have to stay grounded in the truth we've discovered."

Amara nodded, but the weight of the unknown pressed heavily on her. She could feel the gathering storm, could sense that the world was about to be tested in ways none of them had imagined. But she didn't know if she was strong enough to face it. The unveiling had shown her the threads that connected everything, but now those threads felt fragile, as if they could unravel at any moment.

It was a Wednesday evening when the first real sign appeared.

Amara was sitting on her balcony, watching the sunset, when she felt it—an intense wave of energy that hit her like a physical force. Her breath caught in her throat, and she gripped the edge of her chair, her heart racing. The world around her seemed to shift, the colors of the sunset blurring, the air vibrating with something powerful and unsettling.

She closed her eyes, trying to focus, to ground herself, but the energy was overwhelming. It was unlike anything she had felt before—dark and heavy, but also chaotic, like a storm brewing just beneath the surface of the world.

Kael's presence came to her then, calm and steady, anchoring her in the midst of the swirling energy.

"Amara, you need to stay grounded," Kael's voice came, firm but reassuring. **"The shift is happening now. You must be ready."**

Amara's eyes flew open, her pulse quickening. "What is it? What's happening?"

Kael's presence remained steady beside her. **"The balance is shifting. Darkness and light are in conflict. You've seen the threads that connect everything, but now those threads are being tested. The world is on the verge of transformation, but not all forces wish to see it heal."**

Amara's heart raced as Kael's words sank in. The storm she had felt building—the storm they had all felt—was here.

"What do we do?" she asked, her voice trembling.

"You hold the light," Kael said simply. **"You've learned how to face your own darkness. Now you must help others face theirs. The world is waking up, but with that awakening comes fear, doubt, and resistance. You are here to guide, to help those who are lost find their way."**

Amara's breath caught in her throat. She had always known this moment would come, but now that it was here, the weight of it felt overwhelming.

"How do I help?" she whispered.

Kael's voice was soft but filled with conviction. **"By being who you are. By trusting that the light within you is enough. The world needs you now, Amara. The people around you will need your strength, your calm. You've prepared for this. You are ready."**

That night, Amara couldn't sleep. The energy from the evening still buzzed in her veins, leaving her restless and on edge. She could feel the shift, feel the balance of the world tipping, and it left her with a sense of urgency she couldn't shake.

She texted Ethan, needing to connect with someone who understood what she was going through. His reply came quickly: **"I feel it too. We need to meet."**

They agreed to meet at the park the next morning, and as Amara lay in bed, staring up at the ceiling, she felt the weight of what was happening settle over her. The world was changing, and she was part of that change. But what exactly was coming, she still didn't know.

The next morning, the city felt different. As Amara walked to the park, the usual hum of the streets, the rush of people heading to work, all seemed muted, like the world was holding its breath. The sky was overcast, thick clouds hanging low, casting a gray pallor over everything.

When she arrived at the park, Ethan was already there, sitting on the familiar bench by the pond. His face was drawn, his eyes shadowed with worry.

"You feel it too, don't you?" Amara asked as she sat down beside him.

Ethan nodded, his jaw tight. "It's like the air is different. Everything feels... off."

They sat in silence for a moment, both of them staring out at the water. Amara could feel the tension in the air, the sense that something was about to break. The calm before the storm.

"What do we do?" she asked finally, her voice barely above a whisper.

Ethan didn't answer right away, his gaze distant. "We stay grounded. We do what Kael and Liora have been teaching us. We hold the light."

Amara nodded, but the fear still lingered at the edges of her mind. It was one thing to talk about holding the light, but how were they supposed to do that when the world around them was falling apart?

As if reading her thoughts, Ethan turned to her, his expression serious. "We're not alone in this, Amara. You know that. Whatever's coming, we face it together."

Amara looked into his eyes, and for the first time that morning, she felt a spark of hope. He was right. They weren't alone. They had the circle, they had each other, and they had the strength they had built through their journey.

But even as she clung to that hope, the weight of the unknown pressed down on her. The storm was coming. She could feel it in every fiber of her being.

And when it came, they would need every bit of strength they had.

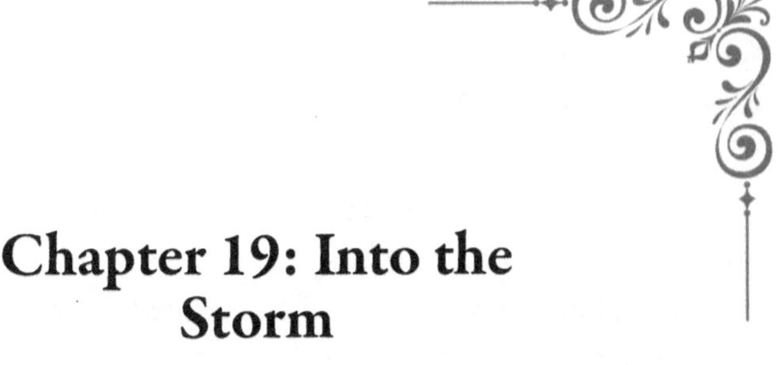

Chapter 19: Into the Storm

The days that followed were filled with a tense, quiet anticipation. Amara and the rest of the circle felt the energy shift growing stronger with each passing moment, as though the world itself was on the verge of tipping into something unknown. The city had taken on an eerie stillness. People moved about their daily routines, but something had changed. There was a restlessness in the air, a sense of unease that no one could quite explain.

Amara could feel it pulsing beneath the surface of everything she did. At work, in the park, even in her quiet moments of meditation, the energy was there—building, waiting, like the calm before a storm. She had done everything Kael and Liora had taught her, staying grounded, trusting in her purpose. But with each passing day, the weight of the coming storm grew heavier, and Amara wondered how long she could hold onto the light she had worked so hard to cultivate.

The circle met more frequently now, gathering in the evenings to meditate, to ground themselves in the collective energy they had been building. Each meeting felt more urgent than the last. Liora guided them through the meditations, her voice calm but filled with an underlying tension.

"We are being tested," Liora said one evening as they sat in a circle, the candlelight casting flickering shadows on the walls. "The energy you feel, the chaos you sense—it is part of the awakening. The world is waking up, and with that awakening comes resistance. Not everyone is ready to face the truth."

Amara listened, her hands resting in her lap, her heart racing. She had known this was coming, had felt the storm gathering for weeks. But now, it felt closer than ever.

"What kind of resistance?" Ethan asked, his brow furrowed.

Liora's gaze was steady as she looked at him. "Fear. Doubt. The forces that have kept the world in darkness for so long. As we awaken, we are disrupting that balance, and the darkness will fight to maintain its hold."

Amara swallowed hard. She had faced her own darkness, but this felt different. This wasn't just about her anymore—it was about the world. The unveiling had shown her the threads that connected everyone, and now those threads were being tested. The storm wasn't just within her—it was everywhere.

"What do we do?" Amara asked softly, her voice trembling.

Liora smiled gently. "We do what we've always done. We hold the light. We trust in our connection to one another, to the universe. This storm will pass, but we must stay strong."

That night, Amara lay awake in bed, staring at the ceiling as the storm raged inside her mind. She had spent so long preparing for this moment, but now that it was here, the weight of it felt overwhelming. The visions she had seen, the unveiling, the lessons Kael had taught her—it was all leading to this. But still, the fear lingered, whispering at the edges of her consciousness.

You're not strong enough.

The thought crept into her mind, uninvited, a remnant of the darkness she had faced in the past. She squeezed her eyes shut, taking a deep breath, trying to push it away. She had come too far to fall back into those patterns now.

But the storm inside her wouldn't be silenced so easily.

She sat up, wrapping her arms around her knees, her heart pounding in her chest. The room felt too small, too quiet, the darkness pressing in on her. For a moment, she felt like she was drowning, the weight of the world's fear and chaos crashing over her, pulling her under.

"You are not alone."

Kael's voice came to her then, steady and reassuring, cutting through the noise in her mind. She could feel his presence beside her, warm and comforting, grounding her in the midst of the chaos.

"You've felt the storm coming," Kael said softly. "But remember, you are not facing it alone. You have the light within you, and you have the people who stand beside you. Together, you will weather this storm."

Amara nodded, her breath coming in slow, steady waves as Kael's presence filled the room. He was right. She wasn't alone. She had her circle, her guides, and the strength she had built over the course of her journey.

But still, the fear lingered, its shadow hovering just beyond her reach.

"What if I'm not strong enough?" she whispered, her voice barely audible.

Kael's presence remained steady. **"You are stronger than you know. You've faced your darkness before, and you will face it again. But you do not have to do it alone. Trust in the light within you, and trust in those who stand with you."**

The following morning, Amara woke with a sense of calm she hadn't expected. The fear from the night before still clung to her, but Kael's words had settled deep within her, a quiet reassurance that anchored her as she moved through the day.

She met Ethan later that evening, and together they walked through the park, the air cool and crisp as the sun dipped below the horizon. They didn't talk much, but the silence between them felt comforting. They were both on edge, both aware that the storm was drawing closer, but there was also a sense of solidarity between them, a shared understanding that whatever was coming, they would face it together.

As they sat on the familiar bench by the pond, Ethan broke the silence. "Do you think we're ready?"

Amara looked at him, her eyes searching his. "I don't know. But I think we have to be."

Ethan nodded, his gaze distant. "Liora said something at the last meeting that's been stuck in my head," he said after a moment. "She said that the world is waking up, but not everyone is ready for that. Do you think... do you think some people will fight it? That they'll try to hold onto the old way of things?"

Amara sighed, her hands fidgeting in her lap. "I think so. People are afraid of change, and this kind of awakening... it's going to force people to look at things they don't want to see. Not everyone is going to be ready for that."

Ethan was quiet for a long time, his eyes fixed on the water. "What if we're not ready for it either?" he asked softly, his voice filled with doubt.

Amara's heart clenched at the vulnerability in his voice. She had asked herself the same question so many times over the past few weeks. But now, sitting here with Ethan, she realized that being ready didn't mean having all the answers. It didn't mean being free of fear.

"We're as ready as we can be," she said gently. "And we're not doing this alone."

That night, Amara dreamed again. But this time, the dream was different.

She stood in the middle of a vast field, the sky above her dark and stormy. The wind howled around her, pulling at her clothes, and the air was thick with the weight of something she couldn't quite name. But unlike the dreams of darkness she had experienced before, this time, she wasn't afraid.

In the distance, she saw others—people she knew, people from the circle, and people she had never met. They stood scattered across the field, their faces filled with the same sense of determination she felt rising inside her.

They were all part of this storm, all part of the awakening. And as the wind whipped around them, they stood strong, their feet planted firmly on the ground.

Kael's voice echoed in her mind, soft but clear. **"The storm is here. But you are ready."**

Amara woke with a start, her body drenched in sweat, her heart pounding in her chest. The room was dark, but the calm from the dream lingered in her mind, steadying her breath.

The storm was here. But she was ready.

Chapter 20: You Are Ready

The storm had arrived.

Amara could feel it in every part of her being. The subtle shifts, the growing tension, the energy that had been building for weeks—it all culminated in this moment. The world around her pulsed with a force she couldn't ignore, and the air felt thick with the weight of everything that had been set in motion.

But now, standing at the threshold of something immense, she was calm. There was fear, yes, but it was no longer overwhelming. The fear had become a companion, something she could carry without letting it control her. The lessons Kael had taught her, the wisdom Liora had shared, the strength of the circle—all of it was with her. And now, it was time to step into the storm, fully awake, fully present.

It was early evening when the final gathering of the circle took place. Liora had called them together, her message brief but urgent: **"It's time."**

Amara arrived at the park with Ethan by her side. They didn't speak as they walked through the trees, their footsteps quiet on the gravel path. There was a stillness in the air, as though the entire world was holding its breath. The usual sounds of the city—the hum of traffic, the distant chatter of people—seemed far away, muted by the energy swirling around them.

When they reached the clearing, the rest of the circle was already there, seated in a circle by the pond. The familiar sight of the group, the warm glow of candlelight flickering between them, filled Amara with a sense of comfort and belonging. They had all felt the shift, all sensed the storm. And now, they would face it together.

Liora stood at the center of the circle, her eyes closed, her hands raised to the sky. Her presence was calm, grounded, and Amara could see the light that radiated from her, even in the dimming evening.

"We are here," Liora said softly, her voice carrying through the stillness. "We have prepared for this moment. The world is changing, and we are part of that change. But tonight, we are not here to resist the storm. We are here to become it."

Amara's breath caught in her throat. **To become the storm.**

Liora's eyes opened, and she looked around the circle, her gaze filled with a quiet strength. "We are the light in the darkness. But we are also the darkness. Both are necessary. Both are part of the awakening."

The words sent a shiver through Amara. She had spent so long fearing the darkness, so long trying to push it away. But now, she understood. The storm wasn't something to be fought—it was something to be embraced. The darkness was not her enemy. It was part of her journey.

Liora gestured for them to join her in the center of the circle, and one by one, they stood and formed a tight ring, hands clasped together, their energy weaving through the space between them.

Amara closed her eyes, feeling the warmth of Ethan's hand in hers, the steady pulse of the energy connecting them all. The world outside the circle faded, and all that remained was the hum of their collective presence, the quiet strength they had built together.

The energy shifted.

It started as a soft ripple, a vibration that hummed through the ground beneath their feet, through the air around them. Amara could feel it deep in her chest, a pulse that seemed to sync with her own heartbeat, growing stronger with each breath she took.

And then, the storm came.

Not with wind or rain, but with a surge of energy that pulsed through the circle, filling them with light, with darkness, with everything they had been preparing for. It was overwhelming, but not in a way that frightened her. The force of it rushed through Amara's veins, expanding outward, connecting her to the others, to the world beyond the circle, to the unseen web that held the universe together.

Visions flashed before her eyes—the unveiling she had witnessed before, but now, more vivid, more alive. She saw the threads that connected them all, glowing with the energy of the storm. She saw the world shifting, people waking up, the light and the darkness weaving together in perfect balance. There was chaos, yes, but there was also peace, a sense of order beneath the surface.

This was the awakening.

The world was changing, and they were part of that change. The old ways were crumbling, and something new was being born. Amara could feel it in every part of her being—the transformation, the rebirth of the world around her.

She wasn't just witnessing the storm. She was the storm. They all were.

As the energy surged through the circle, Amara felt a deep sense of peace settle over her. The fear that had clung to her for so long, the doubt that had whispered in the back of her mind, was gone. In its place was a quiet certainty, a knowing that everything she had experienced, everything she had faced, had led to this moment.

Kael's voice came to her then, soft and steady, as it always had been. **"You are the light, and you are the darkness. You are the storm, and you are the calm that follows. Trust in what you have become, Amara. The world is ready, and so are you."**

Amara's heart swelled with emotion. She could feel Kael's presence with her, as strong as ever, but she knew now that she didn't need his guidance in the same way she once had. He had shown her the path, but it was her journey to walk.

The light within her burned bright, and the darkness flowed through her in equal measure. She was whole.

When the storm passed, the circle was silent. The energy had quieted, but the connection remained. They stood there, hands still clasped, their breathing slow and steady as they came back to themselves.

Amara opened her eyes, blinking against the fading light of the evening. The world around her seemed brighter, more vivid, as though everything had been washed clean by the storm. She looked at Ethan, who was still holding her hand, and smiled. He smiled back, his eyes filled with the same sense of wonder she felt.

They had faced the storm. And they had become it.

Liora stepped forward, her eyes filled with pride as she looked at the group. "This is the beginning," she said softly. "The awakening is here, and the world will never be the same. But you are ready. You've always been ready."

Amara's heart swelled with gratitude, with love for the people who had walked this path with her. She didn't know what the future held, but she knew that they would face it together.

The storm had come, and they had emerged stronger, more connected, more alive than ever before.

That night, as Amara lay in bed, the peace from the evening still wrapped around her like a blanket, she thought about everything she had learned. The journey had been long, filled with darkness and light, with fear and hope. But she had come through it stronger, more whole.

She had become the storm, and now, she would help others do the same.

The world was changing, but Amara was no longer afraid of what was to come.

She was ready.

Lessons from the Realms

As the storm quiets and the light and darkness find their balance, the whispers from the realms leave behind their most important message—one meant for all who seek truth, purpose, and peace. The spirits, our unseen guides, speak not in riddles or secrets, but in the language of the heart. They remind us that the journey of the soul is eternal, woven into the fabric of the universe, and that each step we take is part of a greater plan.

The first lesson they offer is one of unity. We are all connected—through the threads of light, through the shadows we cast, through the lives we touch. No soul stands alone. We are part of a web that stretches beyond time and space, one where each action ripples outward, affecting the whole. To embrace this is to understand that in helping others heal, we heal ourselves. **The individual path is not separate from the collective journey.** When one person awakens, it sends out waves of light that have the power to transform the world.

The second lesson is that light and darkness are not enemies. They are partners in creation, dancing through the realms to maintain balance. Darkness teaches us resilience, strength, and humility. It is only by walking through the shadow that we come to truly appreciate the light. Fear, doubt, and suffering are not punishments—they are teachers, showing us where we need to grow, and where we need to heal. **It is in the acceptance of both light and darkness that true growth begins.** We must learn to face our shadows, embrace them, and integrate them into our wholeness.

The third lesson is trust. Trust the path, even when it is unseen. The human mind craves control, but the spirit knows that not all things can be understood from our limited perspective. There is a plan for each of us, a purpose that unfolds as we move forward. **Trust in divine timing and the unseen forces that guide you.** Even in moments of confusion, *know that you are being led toward the experiences your soul needs for its growth. What may seem like a delay or a loss is often a redirection toward something more aligned with your higher self.*

__The fourth lesson is responsibility.__ We are each responsible for the energy we bring into the world. Our thoughts, words, and actions create ripples that shape the reality around us. The spirits urge us to be mindful of our choices, to understand that every action, no matter how small, contributes to the greater whole. __Karma is not punishment but a mirror, reflecting back to us the energy we put out into the world.__ By acting with integrity, compassion, and love, we create a cycle of positive energy that benefits everyone we encounter.

__The fifth lesson is surrender.__ There are times when we must surrender to the flow of life, to the wisdom of the universe, and to forces beyond our control. Surrender is not about giving up—it is about letting go of the need to force outcomes and trusting that what is meant for us will unfold in perfect timing. __In surrender, we find peace, even in uncertainty.__ The spirits remind us that resistance often creates more suffering, but by releasing our grip and allowing life to flow, we open ourselves to greater possibilities.

__The sixth lesson is that the physical world is temporary, but the spirit is eternal.__ The human experience is but one chapter in the soul's infinite journey. Life on Earth is a classroom where we learn lessons of love, forgiveness, and compassion. The spirits urge us to see beyond the material world and recognize the deeper truths of existence. __What we do here matters, but it is not the end.__ The soul continues, evolving and expanding in ways we cannot fully comprehend. Death is not an ending, but a transition—a return to the greater whole.

__The seventh lesson is about forgiveness.__ Forgiveness is not for others alone, but for ourselves. __Holding onto anger, resentment, or guilt binds us to the very pain we wish to release.__ The spirits remind us that forgiveness is the path to freedom, to letting go of the burdens we carry. By forgiving ourselves and others, we create space for healing and growth.

True forgiveness is an act of love that allows us to release the past and embrace the present with an open heart.

The eighth lesson is that love is the most powerful force in the universe. *Love is the essence of the spirit world, the thread that binds all things together.* **It is not just an emotion, but a state of being, a force that transcends realms.** *The spirits remind us that love is the key to unlocking our true potential, to healing ourselves and the world around us. Love is patient, unconditional, and infinite. To live in love is to live in alignment with the universe, with the highest version of ourselves.*

The ninth lesson is about service. *Our purpose is not just to awaken for ourselves, but to serve others.* **In helping others rise, we fulfill our highest calling.** *The spirits encourage us to extend our hands, to uplift those around us, and to offer our light where it is needed most. Whether through small acts of kindness or grand gestures, we all have the power to make a difference.* **Service is the way we contribute to the healing of the collective soul.**

The final lesson is about presence. *Life happens in the now. The past is gone, and the future is uncertain, but the present moment is where all transformation occurs.* **The spirits ask us to be fully present in our lives, to engage with the world around us, and to embrace each moment as sacred.** *In presence, we find peace. In presence, we discover who we truly are.*

The spirits from the realms want the world to know this: **You are more powerful than you know. You are a beacon of light in the darkest moments, and your purpose is not just to survive, but to awaken, to heal, and to help others find their way.**

The storm may rage, but within you is the calm. Within you is the light.

And that light can never be extinguished.

Don't miss out!

Visit the website below and you can sign up to receive emails whenever AMEYA VATSA publishes a new book. There's no charge and no obligation.

https://books2read.com/r/B-A-BNMKC-XGYZE

BOOKS 2 READ

Connecting independent readers to independent writers.

Did you love *Whispers from the Realms*? Then you should read *Girl veiled by Time* by AMEYA VATSA!

When Finn stumbles upon a hidden village deep in the countryside, it feels like the escape he's been searching for—a place untouched by time, full of quiet beauty and mystery. With no trace of the contemporary world, the village offers Finn a fresh start, far from the problems of his old life. But what begins as a peaceful retreat quickly turns into something far more sinister.

At the heart of it all is Elara, an enigmatic woman who seems to be tied to the village in ways Finn can't quite understand. Her allure is undeniable, yet she holds secrets beneath her calm exterior. People whisper of things they refuse to explain, shadows lurk just out of sight, and Finn starts to question the very reality around him.

The village holds countless secrets—hidden pasts, forgotten rituals, and strange forces that seem to govern the lives of those who stay. As the ground beneath Finn's feet begins to shift, he's thrust into a race against time to uncover the truth. What is this place? Why was he drawn here?

About the Author

Ameya Vatsa, legally known as **Ankita Kumari**, is an author who explores themes of spiritual awakening, personal transformation, and the deeper mysteries of existence. Drawing from both personal experiences and spiritual insights, Ameya weaves intricate tales that resonate with readers seeking more than just entertainment—those who yearn for understanding and connection.

When not writing, Ankita enjoys reading, painting, and collecting real stories, continually finding inspiration in both the seen and unseen world.